Janet Quin-Harkin

Janet Quin-Harkin is better known these days as New York Times bestselling author Rhys Bowen, writer of the historical *Molly Murphy* and *Royal Spyness* mystery series. She has won the Agatha Best Novel Award and was nominated for the Edgar Best Novel. In the eighties, when this series was written, she was dubbed by one newspaper as "the Queen of Teen Romance." Janet/Rhys is a transplanted Brit who now divides her time between California and Arizona. You can visit her website at www.rhysbowen.com

JANET QUIN-HARKIN

Heartbreak
═ *Café* ═

1

NO EXPERIENCE
REQUIRED

ELLINGSTAR
M E D I A

www.Ellingstar.com

An Ellingstar Book

First published in America by Fawcett Books, New York in 1989
First published in Great Britain by Armada in 1989
Reprinted in Great Britain by Diamond books in 1994
This paperback edition published in 2014 by Ellingstar Media

alloy**entertainment**

Published by arrangement with Rights People, London

A CIP Catalogue record for this book is available from the British Library

ISBN 978-0-9929330-0-5

Typeset by M Rules

Printed and bound in by CPI Group (UK) Ltd, Croydon, CR0 4YY

This book is made from Forest Stewardship Council™ certified paper.

Ellingstar Media Ltd.
37 Warren Street, London W1T 6AD
www.Ellingstar.com

www.HeartbreakCafe.LA

1989

1989

Chapter One

I remember the first time I saw the Heartbreak Café – really noticed it, I mean. I must have driven past it a thousand times on my way to the beach with my friends. But on this particular fall day, Grant – my boyfriend – had taken me out in his new sports car, which had been a seventeenth birthday present. After a thrilling drive along the clifftop road, we ended up at Rockley Beach. Grant suggested we get a soda or something to celebrate his car, but it was Sunday and all the trendy beachfront cafes were full of middle-aged people who'd come out from the city. There were even people waiting for tables, and Grant hates to wait for anything. So do I, for that matter.

After we had tried every cafe and given up in disgust, we headed back to Grant's car, which was parked at least three blocks away because of the Sunday traffic. That's when we saw the Heartbreak. It was nestled in behind the ritzy, beachfront boutiques, among a bunch of old fishermen's cottages. It must have once been a fisherman's cottage itself because it still looked like one – wooden front porch and all – but a neon sign in the window said Heartbreak Café, and there was loud music coming from inside. Grant took in the cafe's peeling paint, the music, and the motorcycles and beat-up cars with surfboards strapped to their roofs parked around it.

"This isn't our sort of place," he said, and firmly took my hand and led me back to the car.

I didn't give much thought to Rockley Beach or the Heartbreak for a while after that. Little matters like my junior year in school, with tons of chemistry and trig homework, plus a leading role in our school production of *Bye Bye Birdie*, kept me more than occupied all winter anyway. The boys just said it was no fun to surf in cold water, but secretly I think they were scared of the gigantic waves that came after each storm. You had to be brave or crazy, or both, to want to ride those waves, and my friends were all pretty sane and sensible – when it came to surfing, at least.

The second time I noticed the Heartbreak, one afternoon in late April, I hadn't actually intended to drive down to Rockley at all. I had been heading for the Hillsdale Mall for some major shopping-therapy, but my head was still so full of the fight I'd just had with my mother that I missed my turning. Before I knew it I was driving down the winding, narrow canyon that led to the beach. It's impossible to turn round on that road, so I just kept on going. Then, when I saw the sun glistening on the ocean, I decided a walk on the beach might not be such a bad idea. It sure was cheaper than the mall, which was a definite plus now that I could no longer count on an allowance from either one of my parents.

Recollecting my present poverty brought back all the details of my fight with Mom earlier that afternoon. Before the divorce we hardly ever had fights at home. My parents were the sort of people who liked to reason things through. "Now, Debbie, let's just sit down and approach this in a mature fashion ...," they'd begin. It used to infuriate me at times. They were always so calm and rational. I guess that's why the split up came as a complete surprise. Other kids knew months beforehand that something was wrong because of all the yelling and stomping out of the house. I didn't know anything until the day my father moved out. But to be fair to my folks, I don't think they were even sure they were getting a divorce until Dad moved out.

I was generally pretty happy with the way things were, and I assumed my parents were, too. But it turned out that my father hadn't been happy for some time. At least that's what he said in the letter he wrote me after he left. He'd always dreamed of being a writer, he wrote, and his life with us left him no time and space to be himself. So now he was off, being himself presumably, and Mom and I were still wondering what had happened to us.

I thought my mother took it very well, considering that one day she was June Cleaver and the next she was a single parent. She was still calm and controlled when she spoke to me about our future.

I tried to be calm and controlled too, at first, but it just didn't work. My parents decided to sell our house and split the profits so that they both could have something to live on until my mom got a job and my dad started selling his screenplays. It didn't take a genius to realize that we'd be living somewhere pretty crummy if they wanted the money from the house as profits and not as a new house. I hadn't seen the artists' settlement where Dad was living. Mom and I moved into a disgusting condo. I mean, it wasn't literally disgusting: it didn't have roaches all over the floor or anything. But it was in a big condo project – "The Oaks, A Planned Community for Today's Family". The planning consisted of an imaginative arrangement of lookalike condos in stick-straight rows. Only the fake Spanish beams round the windows and the circles of artfully-placed junipers and rocks prevented it from looking like a planned prison.

When I objected my mother claimed it was perfectly adequate for the two of us and she liked knowing that the place was patrolled by security guards. Then she gave me another speech about "making the best of things". It wasn't as if I had to change schools or anything, she said. And the place had a pool and tennis courts, not so different from the country club we'd always belonged to. Although her arguments weren't convincing, I tried to stop complaining. It wasn't really my mother's fault that we were there, and she probably felt bad about it, too, inside.

So life went on. My dad told me I could come over and visit him any time, once he got settled, and my mom said that was fine with her, so I guessed I was pretty lucky – as lucky as a person can be who has just moved out of a big, beautiful house, lost her country club membership, and sold all her matching bedroom furniture – including the canopy bed – because her new bedroom is too small for anything other than a hideous teak module.

My life was still full of school and after-school activities, and, best of all, dates with my boyfriend Grant. Even after a year together, I still couldn't get over Grant. I still didn't really understand why one of the best-looking, most outstanding guys in the whole school had noticed me at the cast party after last year's play. Having a boyfriend who was a popular senior was one of the few things that had really gone right for me the whole year. I'd be going to senior ball and all sorts of good stuff – if we could still afford to buy me a prom dress, that is!

So having Grant around and looking forward to all the pre-graduation events kept me going. Meanwhile, my mother got dressed up in a suit every day and started looking for a job, circling ads in the paper and making the rounds of employment agencies. I thought it would only be a matter of time before she became Mrs Modern Executive, earning the same sort of salary my father had, and things returned to normal again. So I was hardly prepared for what happened on that April afternoon. I had just poured myself a glass of juice when my mother came in, waving a letter at me.

"Deborah," she said, "this came today and we have to talk about it."

I opened the envelope. "What is it?" I asked, trying to make sense of the columns of figures.

"It's your bill for your car insurance."

"Oh." I stared at it, wondering what I was supposed to say next. "What am I supposed to do with it?" I asked finally.

"Someone's got to pay it," she said.

I looked at it again. "It's six hundred dollars," I said with a laugh. This had to be a joke.

"Right," Mom said. She was not smiling.

"I don't have six hundred dollars."

"Neither do I."

"So what do we do?" I asked.

She sighed. "I wish I knew," she said. "Any suggestions?"

"How should I know what to do?" I asked. I could feel my face getting hot because I wasn't sure what she was getting at.

She looked at me steadily. She had the "Let's be mature and reasonable" look on her face. "Deborah, up to now your father and I have always shielded you from the unpleasant things in life," she said. "Now you are going to have to face facts. It costs money to run a car. I can hardly afford to pay for my own car. Yours is a luxury we might have to do without."

"*WE* might have to do without?" I asked, my voice rising dangerously. "I notice you are not the one volunteering to do without a car."

"Be reasonable," she said. "I need a car if I'm going to get a job."

"And I don't need a car to go to school? There isn't exactly a good public transportation system round here, you know. You want me to hitchhike to school, is that it?"

"Deborah, when I was your age—" she began.

I interrupted her. "Great. Now I'm going to get the speech about how you had to walk five miles to school in the snow, uphill both ways ..."

She didn't smile.

I could feel a lump form at the back of my throat.

"How can I pay for it?" I demanded. "You bought me a car as a present. You didn't mention anything about having to pay for its upkeep then ..."

"Things have changed ..."

"You can say that again!" I shouted. "I get my house taken away, my father taken away, my bedroom set taken away, and now you want to take my car, too!"

"Do you think I'm having a picnic?" my mother demanded. She was beginning to yell, too, and my mother *never* yelled. "You think it's just fine and dandy going to interviews with twenty-three-year-old girls who fling my resume back in my face and tell me I don't have any experience? I am not exactly thrilled about getting a job, but I'm looking for one. Maybe you should, too!"

"You want me to get a job, is that what you're saying?" I yelled. "You don't care suddenly about my school work or plays or the debate club or anything, right?"

"Of course I care," she said, her voice cracking, "but we can't always have what we want, can we?" Her face was all screwed up and angry, like I'd never seen it before. "I'm just saying you're going to have to share some of the responsibilities round here because right now I've got too many!"

I started to walk towards the door. "Fine, if that's what you want, I'll get a job. I'll go out and look for one right now. I'm sure they need people on the night shift in the mines. Or maybe I can find myself a job at the Playboy Club – that doesn't conflict with school hours."

Then I ran out of the front door and jumped into my car before I started crying. I put my foot down and drove fast after that, heading, as I usually did when I was depressed, to the shopping mall. I don't know what I'd intended to buy with my rapidly-dwindling bank balance. But I guess my eyes were more fuzzy with tears than I thought because I was halfway down the canyon before I noticed I had missed my turning and was heading towards destiny in the form of the Heartbreak Café.

Chapter Two

At least seeing Rockley Beach took my mind off my gloomy thoughts. It was always pretty, but that afternoon it looked especially beautiful – like a setting for a movie. Its pastel buildings glowed as if the long winter rains had washed them spring clean. Their windows winked back the afternoon sunlight and the ocean beyond sparkled and glittered, each wave decorated with a frosting of foamy white spray. I slowed down, squinting against the fierce sunlight reflecting off the ocean and started looking for a parking place. The only trouble was I was not the only person who thought Rockley Beach might be a good place to visit on a bright spring afternoon. Every space along the little main street was taken, some by old clunkers belonging to surfing nuts who were taking advantage of the season's first warm day, and others by BMWs and Mercedes, obviously not driven by surfers. I could see some of their owners walking down on the beach in sensible shoes and tweedy skirts, which was just what I wanted to do right now – walk on the beach, that is, not wear tweedy skirts. I began to face the fact that there might not be a parking space for me and I'd have to drive back up the canyon again. It seemed like the afternoon was doomed, whatever I did.

As I turned from the beachfront and began to drive back along the approach road, I finally saw a parking space. It was in between an old building and a fence, not big enough for one of those big cars, but just the right size for my little Golf convertible.

As I turned I saw the neon sign on the old building and remembered why it looked so familiar. It was the Heartbreak Café. I hesitated for a moment, taking in the fact that I'd have to come in very straight if I didn't want to risk scratching my paintwork. It was also pretty muddy. I had just decided that it was worth going ahead and risking mud splatters when I heard a huge roaring sound and a motorcycle zipped past me into the space. My nerves were so tense by this time that I leaped angrily out of the car, ready to do battle.

"Just what do you think you are doing?" I yelled over the roar of the motorcycle. It occurred to me in midsentence that I was probably yelling at a Hell's Angel and that I should have my head examined. The bike's rider was very large, and dressed all in black leather. With the helmet he was wearing he looked sort of like Darth Vader. If he'd taken his helmet off and turned out to be a green metal robot, I wouldn't have been too surprised. As it was he lifted the flap of his helmet, and I saw dark eyes looking at me in amusement. I suppose I must have looked pretty strange, dancing up and down and flapping my arms.

"What?" he shouted back.

"You took my space!" I shouted. He turned off the bike's engine in midsentence so that I ended up yelling into silence.

He came round his bike towards me. Instead of looking as if he were about to knock me unconscious, he looked surprised.

"How do you figure this space is yours?" he asked.

"I was about to drive into it and you stole it from me!" I yelled. "You could see I was straightening up to get into it."

He looked at me, then back at the space. "Oh, then you must be Miss Patrons," he said seriously.

"I must be what?" I began to wonder if the guy was all there.

He pointed to a sign on the fence which I hadn't seen until then. "It says Space Reserved for Café Patrons," he said with the hint of a grin. "Nice name. Can I call you Cafe or do you prefer Miss Patrons?"

"Very funny," I growled. I glanced at the Heartbreak. There were no lights on inside the building and the notice on the front door read, Open Weekdays – 4 p.m. to midnight. "The cafe's not even open," I said smugly.

"So how do you know I'm not a patron arriving early?" he asked.

"A whole hour early?"

The dark eyes looked at me steadily. "I might be a French fry junkie waiting impatiently for my next fix."

"The same might go for me," I said. "You don't know I'm not a patron arriving early ..."

He looked me over, then shook his head. "No. You're not the type. You belong down there in La Lanterna with the fettuccine and croissants."

I glared at him. "You're not going to move for me, are you?"

He took off his helmet, revealing a mop of unruly dark hair which he combed through with his fingers. "You couldn't park here anyway," he said. "The space is too narrow. You might scratch your nice new paint job."

"For your information, I'm a very good driver," I said. "I haven't scratched this car once."

He grinned at this, a sort of patronizing grin that made me even madder, if that was possible. His eyes lingered on the parking permit on my windshield. "I bet they have nice big spaces over at the country club," he said. "And besides, you'd get mud all over those nice aluminium wheels if you parked here. I'm doing you a favour really."

I didn't know what to do. He obviously was not going to move, and I didn't want just to drive away and let him know he'd won, so we stood staring at each other until the problem was solved for us. My car was still sticking out into traffic, almost blocking the narrow street. Cars began to pile up on either side of me – surfers anxious to get down to the waves in one direction and BMW drivers anxious to get home and cook dinner in the other. Everyone started honking at once.

"I think you'd better be going," the biker said. "They give out tickets for holding up traffic."

I couldn't do anything but growl and mutter under my breath as he watched me back my car into the traffic and get going the right way. It took me a couple of tries because the cars on either side hadn't left me much space. I thought I saw the guy grin when I ground the gears once. "He probably is a patron," I muttered to myself. "He looks like he belongs in that place. I bet it's full of bikers and other lowlife people who steal parking spaces. If I'd parked there he probably would have stolen my hub caps or slashed my tyres, so I'm lucky really that I got out of there ..." I kept on muttering, but it didn't do much good. I was still mad and super-tense by the time I saw a car back out of a perfectly good, large, clean parking space. I parked the Golf there.

My spirits revived a little when I saw that the person before me had left almost an hour on the meter. By the time I got down to the beach and kicked off my shoes in the soft sand, I had almost put the parking-space incident out of my mind, leaving plenty of room for the big worry of the day: how to pay for my car insurance. One thing was certain, I was not going to give up that little car. My folks had promised me a car when I got my licence, but I had expected something safe and ordinary – not a cute, zippy little convertible. My dad must have chosen it. He liked things to be fun as well as functional. My mother hadn't been so sure, even from the start. She kept reminding me that convertibles are easy targets for theft and that the engine was very powerful and that I'd get ear infections if I drove with the top down in the winter.

Mom was the type who always went for safety over glamour. And now she was suggesting that I sell it, as if it didn't matter to me at all!

"Sorry, Mom, but I'm not about to give up the one thing I've got left," I muttered as I strode out down the beach. "You want me to get a job, I'll get a job!"

My mind instantly ran through scenes of various career choices my mother would regret forcing me to make. I saw myself up to my armpits in greasy water as I worked my way through ceiling-high piles of dishes, as a maid sweeping floors, as a stable hand shovelling muck from the stables, until I settled on a dramatic black-and-white scene of myself in the worst kind of sweatshop: I was at a sewing machine in a room full of whirring, clattering machines. The noise level was terrible, the heat was terrible, and the whole place was lit by one naked lightbulb. Beads of perspiration ran down my face, which was grey with exhaustion as I tried to get through my quota of overalls, my fingers raw from the coarse fabric. I squinted as my mother came to find me, my eyes weakened from severe strain. "I got a job like you told me, Mom," I murmured through cracked, parched lips (we only had one break in a ten-hour shift). "I guess you're happy now ..."

This last scene was so ridiculous that I had to laugh. I'd always been famous among my family and friends for overdramatizing. When I was little and I cut my finger and nobody paid any attention, I pretended to faint in the middle of the sidewalk. When my fifth- grade teacher was mean to me, I used to picture the school catching fire and I was the only person who could save this teacher, who'd be stuck up on the roof. Would I save her or leave her to burn? I used to end that scene in different ways depending on how mean she'd been.

You dummy, I told myself. *There is nothing so strange about getting an after-school job! Plenty of kids do it. There are fast food restaurants and movie theatres* ... I cheered up at this thought. Working at a movie theatre wouldn't be bad at all. I'd probably get to see all the movies free.

Maybe I'd swing by the big theatre complex at the mall on my way home ...

I stood at the edge of the ocean and let the waves ripple over my feet. The water was still ice cold. Crazy surfers in wetsuits were way out there, riding the big ones in. As I watched, one guy wiped out. His board flipped up in the air as he disappeared beneath the spray. I shivered and turned away, glad I wasn't with him. *Maybe I'm more like Mom than Dad, after all,* I thought. *Maybe I like to play it safe and not take risks* ...

I ran back up the beach, sending up a shower of sand behind me, and sat on the stone wall to brush off my feet before putting my shoes on again. Then I headed back to my car. When I passed the Heartbreak Café, I couldn't help glancing across to see if the motorcycle was still in my parking space. The bike was there all right, but there was no sign of the rider. Lights were on in the windows of the Heartbreak. There was also a notice in the window that I swear was not there earlier. It read: Wanted —Part-Time Help.

I couldn't help smiling. Imagine my mother's face if I went home and told her I'd got a job as a waitress at a biker hangout! That would be almost as good as the job in the sweatshop. But I was suddenly curious to see inside the place. Avoiding the pot-holes and mud puddles, I walked across the parking lot and peeked in the window. It turned out that the windows were too high to offer a good view, but from what I could see, the place was still deserted. I went up the steps on to the porch and tried the front door. It was open, and I stepped cautiously inside, but no one was there.

The Heartbreak Café wasn't exactly what I had expected. I had expected, well, something sleazy, but this was just simple. It smelled slightly of hamburgers and fries, but there was nothing greasy spoon about it. The interior walls of the former cottage had been knocked out to form one big room, except for a wall with a counter cut into it, which, I figured, must hide the kitchen. With the evening sunlight streaming in through the two west-facing windows, it seemed friendly and sleepy. At the front, beside the counter, was a table holding ketchup, napkins, and all that sort of stuff. On the far wall was an enormous jukebox, straight out of the '50s, but that was the only decoration. No candles or flowers on the tables, no pictures on the walls, except for a chart showing the dates of last fall's Harbor High football games and a torn poster of a surfer riding a wave. The tables were of plain polished wood, with wooden benches on either side. In the corners garden trellises made little booths and their seats were red leather. At the very back were two old sofas facing each other across a coffee table with a half-finished Monopoly game on it. I began to feel like the Prince discovering Sleeping Beauty's castle. I half expected to find the café's occupants asleep under cobwebs.

I was lost in these thoughts when someone spoke right behind me, making me jump a mile. I backed into a bench and almost landed on the floor.

"We're closed!" the voice growled. "Can't you read?" With my heart still hammering I turned to see an old man leaning on the counter, looking out at me with an unfriendly scowl. He had a mop of iron-grey hair, eyebrows as thick and spiky as fresh prawns, and big, heavy jowls which made him look like a bad-tempered bulldog. I took a step back towards the door.

"The door was open," I said in my defence. He continued to scowl.

"It ain't four o'clock yet, is it?" he demanded. "If the sign says closed, it means closed." I was about to apologize when I suddenly felt angry instead. After all, if you have a café and you leave the door open, anyone has a right to wander in, don't they? He let out a sort of half-laugh, half-snort.

I had enough of fighting people for one afternoon and decided that nobody, least of all old prawn-brows here, was going to get the better of me again. "I don't see what's so funny," I said, putting on my best we-are-not-amused tone.

He looked me up and down and made the same snorty noise again. "You come about the job?" he asked.

"What's so strange about that? You do have a job advertised in the window, don't you?"

I could see him taking in my linen miniskirt, my designer flats, the big grosgrain bow holding back my hair ...

"Not the type," he said.

"What do you mean, not the type?"

"You look like you'd freak out on me if you broke a fingernail," he commented dryly. "I need someone who's not afraid of hard work."

"I'm not afraid of hard work," I said haughtily.

"Like what?"

"I ... I sold the most boxes of cookies in my Brownie troup!" At least that made him stop scowling and start grinning. *Now he will think I'm totally useless,* I thought. *What on earth made me say that, anyway? It just slipped out in desperation. What an incredibly dumb thing to say – couldn't I think of one thing I'd done since second grade?* I also remembered, but did not say, that the only reason I'd sold the most boxes was that my father took them down to his office. I searched my brain desperately. "I've also, er, I ran the bake sale for the French Club, and I was in charge of the decorations for the Black and White Ball for the Symphony last year ... and I gave blood!" I babbled on, my face getting redder and redder.

He looked up at the ceiling as if to say, can you believe this girl? "This is a café," he said. "People come here to eat. The important thing is, can you cook?"

"I can cook," I said, trying to regain the regal face I lost when I started blabbing about the Brownies.

"What I mean is ...," he said, gesturing with his arms so violently that he almost knocked over a bottle of ketchup, "have you ever cooked for people? Lots of people, all yelling at once for their hamburgers?"

"I was in charge of cooking once at summer camp," I said in a flash of inspiration. I didn't add that what I was actually in charge of was seeing that my cabin was supplied with marshmallows and sticks for the campfire.

He nodded, but I couldn't tell whether he thought this was good or bad. "What about jobs?" he asked. "You never had paying jobs?"

I was aware for the first time that he had a slight foreign accent hidden somewhere in that gruff voice.

"I've done babysitting," I said. "But I never needed a job until now."

"So you think you need this job?" he asked.

"Yes, I do." I said.

He stared at me as if he were trying to read what was going on inside my head. "Why would you want to wash dishes in a café?" he asked with a snorting laugh. "Girls like you get a bigger allowance than I pay. I don't want nobody who's only going to show up when it suits them!"

I stared at him, determined not to lower my eyes in front of those twitching prawn brows. "I wouldn't be asking for the job if I didn't need it," I said bravely, "and I'll show up."

He nodded again, the prawn brows seeming to move up and down with a life of their own. "Spunky little thing, I'll say that for you," he said at last. "What's your name?"

"Debbie," I said. "Debbie Lesley."

"Okay, Debbie Lesley," he said, running the words together so that it sounded like an exotic Italian dish: Eat all your Debbilesli. "I'm Joe Garbarini. I don't think you'll make it, but I'm prepared to give you a try. Can you start tomorrow?"

"I – I guess so," I stammered.

"Okay. Be here at ten. We open at eleven o'clock on weekends," he said.

"Thank you," I said, smiling at him for the first time. "See you tomorrow then."

Outside, I jumped down the three steps from the porch. I felt terrific. I had gone to my first interview and forced somebody to hire me! I had fought and not taken no for an answer and won. Maybe I should give Mom a few tips on how to get a job. It was only when I was halfway back to my car that I realized something: I hadn't wanted this job in the first place!

Chapter Three

My mother wasn't there when I got home. All the way up the canyon I had planned how I was going to burst in yelling, "Guess what? I got a job already. Not bad for one hour's search, eh?"

I did the bursting in all right, but I was met by silence. I went from room to room, which didn't take me long now that we lived in a cereal box, slowly realizing that my mother was indeed not there. She hadn't mentioned anything about going out when I saw her after school, but then we hadn't had much time for normal conversation before we started yelling. I poured myself a glass of fresh orange juice and sat there, feeling unreasonably mad at her for spoiling my surprise. She wanted me to get a job and I went right out and got one, and now she wasn't even around to hear about it! Mothers are supposed to be around when you need them, not going running off without telling anybody.

As it got closer to dinner time, my annoyance turned to worry. Maybe she had gone out looking for me because I was so upset when I left. Perhaps she thought I might have run away or driven my car off a cliff or something. (This was hardly likely considering that I had made quite a few dramatic exits in my time but always came home in time for the next meal. I even ran away a couple of times, once leaving the enigmatic clue, "You'll never find me. I've gone to a place that rhymes with ball!" Since the mall was within walking distance and I spent half my time there anyway, they found me pretty quickly, just as I had hoped they would.) Surely my mother didn't really think I was still young enough to run away, did she?

It got later. My stomach started making noises like you hear in the lion house at feeding time. I opened the fridge to see if I could get dinner started, now that I was an official cook! There wasn't much there – some milk, yoghurt, half a cucumber and some alfalfa sprouts. Hardly the beginnings of a feast. The freezer wasn't much better. There wasn't even a dinner in a box to shove in the microwave.

Perhaps she's gone for Chinese food, I thought hopefully. Mom had been doing that quite a bit since we were on our own. I adored Chinese food and she thought it was very healthful if you left out the egg rolls.

My mouth was watering just thinking about Ta-Chien Chicken when I finally heard the front door open.

"It's about time," I called. "Where's the Lo Mein?"

"The what?" My mother looked confused. "Oh, food! I knew I'd forgotten something. My head was just so full ..."

I stared at her. "You were out until seven o'clock and you didn't even bring home dinner?" I asked bleakly.

"We'll have to make do with what there is," Mom said, taking off her jacket and draping it over the back of a chair, which should have given me a hint right there that something not normal had happened. She was usually a neatness freak.

"What there is?" I said. "There is yoghurt and cucumber. That's hardly a meal for a growing girl."

"It's very healthy, and you stopped growing at sixteen," my mother countered. "Anyway, let's think about food later. Maybe we'll even go out and celebrate ..."

My eyes lit up. "You got a job!" I cried. "Which is terrific because I've also got news for you—"

"I didn't get a job," she cut in. "I went on an interview for a job. I didn't get it."

"Then why are we celebrating?" I asked cautiously. These days conversations with my mother often resembled Alice's chats with the Cheshire Cat or the March Hare.

"Because I made a wonderful decision that will change my whole life!" my mother said, beaming at me.

"What is it?" I asked, still cautious. I was afraid she'd say something weird like she met a man at the employment exchange and they'd decided to get married.

"Well," Mom began, sliding on to one of the kitchen stools and swinging around like a little kid. "After you left I went through the evening paper as usual, looking for jobs. I saw one that seemed just right for me. It was for a publicity assistant for a big company and it was close by. Well, I thought I'd be great at it – after all the publicity work I've done for fashion shows and PTA functions and golf tournaments . . . so I rushed right down there. They almost laughed in my face, Deborah." She paused and looked up at me indignantly. "They told me they needed someone with experience. I argued that I'd had lots of experience, just not paid. They said that unless I'd worked in a similar job for a similar company in this area, they wouldn't even consider me!" She paused again and began playing with a paper napkin I'd left on the counter.

"That's dumb," I said, because I felt some comment was expected of me.

She thumped her hand on the table. "You'd better believe it's dumb!" she said. "I got pretty mad. I asked them how I was supposed to get experience if nobody would hire me, and they said they might have considered me if I had a degree in Marketing or Communications!"

"That's too bad," I said with understanding, having just had to fight my way through an interview too. "And you do too have experience. You used to work before I was born, didn't you?"

She gave a little sigh. "Nobody's interested in sixteen-year-old experience," she said, "besides, those jobs I did back then weren't worth anything. I did filing and other boring stuff like that. Just to keep us going until your father got his law degree. I even waited tables once . . ."

"You did?" I asked with amazement and delight.

She grinned. "In the college cafeteria one semester . . . and I sold fabrics, but no real career-type jobs. Your father never intended me to work. Lawyers' wives didn't in those days . . ." She twisted her stool away from me.

I stepped up behind her. "It's not fair," I said sympathetically. "Unpaid work should count too. You've done great work publicizing things. What about that fashion show you did for the humane society? That was brilliant! And the bowl-a-thon at school raised a lot of money."

She nodded. "But none of them are worth a hill of beans in the real world, honey," she said.

"So?" I insisted. "What are we celebrating then? You found a job you liked better?"

"I was driving home, feeling very down, and I came to the stoplight next to Shoreline College," she explained. "There was this big board lit up outside saying spring quarter classes start this week. Next thing I knew, I found myself driving into the parking lot."

"And?" I asked impatiently.

"I decided right there and then," she said, tossing back her hair exactly the way I do.

"You decided to sign up for some classes," I asked. "That's not a bad idea. I hear they have some great adult-ed classes there."

"I decided to forget the job and go back to school full-time."

"You did what?" I hadn't meant to yell, but I heard my voice bouncing back from those shiny thin walls.

"I decided this might be the time to finish my degree," Mom replied. "After all, I gave up my own education to put your father through law school and look where that got me! I'm unemployable and alone at age thirty-nine."

"Not quite alone," I reminded her. "You've got me."

"But not for long," she said. "Only one more year and you'll be away in college. I've got to think of my future. I don't want to look forward to years of being turned down for humble little jobs I know I could do with one hand behind my back. I'll take their crummy communications and marketing courses and come out waving an MBA at them!"

I looked at her, wondering if an unseen ventriloquist was making my mother's mouth move. This was a woman whose entire ambition in life up till now was to bake the perfect wholewheat bread. She never even wanted to be president of the PTA!

"So how long will this take?" I asked.

She looked up, her eyes bright. "I've been speaking with a counsellor at the college, and he says I need five more quarters for my bachelors, then if I go on to my masters, that will be a couple more years."

"You're going to be a student for almost four years?" I asked. "Where will the money come from?"

"The counsellor says I should get some sort of financial aid since I've got a dependent child," she said, "and we do have the profit from the house. We can live on that for now. Maybe I can fit in a part-time job to keep us going."

A horrible thought just struck me. "And what about my college?" I asked. "What if I get into Stanford or Brown?"

Mom smiled at me encouragingly. "We'll face that hurdle when we come to it," she said. "You may have to go to a community college like mine."

"A community college?" I blurted out. "But I've worked and slaved for three years to get into any college I want! If I'd known I was going to end up with the airheads at Shoreline, I wouldn't have bothered. Maybe I'd have been better off spending my time with them in the girls' rooms getting high!"

"Don't talk that way, Deborah," Mom said. "I'm sure things will work out for you. You're bright, you've studied hard. You might get all sorts of scholarships."

"I might not," I said gloomily. I walked across the kitchen. "I suppose I'd better make us a cucumber salad, since that's the only food in the house – and now that you're going to be a full-time student, I don't suppose it's going to get much better."

My mother slid from her stool. "Don't begrudge me my chance, Debbie, honey," she said. "I'm really looking forward to going back to school. I was going steady with your father when I started college, seeing him every weekend. I never got the feel of school life. There's so much art and literature I missed out on."

I got out the food and remembered my news. "It's okay. You can go back to school," I said, "because I just got a job, so I can support you."

"Deborah, you didn't? Already?" She looked delighted. In fact, she looked like a little kid at a birthday party. I tried to be glad for her, but I could not stop my stomach from feeling as if I'd dropped into an empty elevator shaft and was still waiting to hit bottom. I was Alice back in Wonderland again – in a world where parents were children and children were parents. I was now going to be working while my mother played at literature and arts. Did that make sense? Was that even fair?

"Tell me about your job?" she said, slipping an arm round my shoulder. I brushed it off.

"It's at a greasy spoon cafe where the bikers hang out," I said bluntly.

Mom let out a nervous little laugh. "Stop kidding around. What is it really?"

"Really, truly, Mom," I said, facing her. "Cross my heart and hope to die. I got the first job I saw because I needed it right away. It's a place called the Heartbreak Café, down on the beach, and it's where all the surfing bums and bikers hang out. I'll be doing all the dog's work: waitressing, washing up, cooking French fries ..."

"Oh, come on, Deborah," Mom said, still looking at me as if she didn't quite believe me. "There must be other jobs ..."

"You just said you were a waitress!"

"Yes, but at the college. That was different ... lots of us had to work," she said firmly. "But not that sort of place, Debbie ..."

I refused to discuss it for the rest of the evening, which I could tell was upsetting her. I knew she was waiting for me to start laughing and say, "Ha, ha. Just kidding. I'm really working at a fashion boutique." Or at the library. Someplace appropriate. And I could tell she was still feeling uneasy when I went to bed.

The next morning I showed up, right on the dot of ten, at the Heartbreak. Parking was easy at that hour because most people didn't get going much before lunch on weekends, so I was able to park out of the mud, on the other side of the café. The sun was still shining, the day was warm, and I felt excited – that sort of half-scared, half-looking-forward feeling you get as you go up the first slope on a roller coaster or watch the opening credits to a horror movie. Whatever working at the Heartbreak was like, it was going to be a new experience, and I was anxious to find out how I'd do. On the whole I felt pretty confident: after all there couldn't be too much to remembering "one hamburger and a large fries" or turning over patties, could there? I was determined to show old Mr Garbarini that I wasn't the delicate little rose he obviously thought I was.

I had dressed in my oldest jeans and one of my father's big shirts, determined not to look like a snob. The front door was locked this time. I knocked and Mr Garbarini came round to open it.

"I didn't think you'd show," he said.

"I said I would," I answered, stepping inside. "I always do what I say I will."

"I thought you'd have second thoughts when you got home, maybe deciding that washing dishes and waiting tables were not for you," he said, closing the door behind me.

I didn't tell him that I had had second, third, and even fourth thoughts, but that it was more important for my mother to see me returning exhausted after a day's slavery. Maybe then she'd have second thoughts about all that literature and art and start acting like a mother again. "I said I wasn't afraid of hard work," I answered. "What do you want me to do first?"

"Put on a uniform," he said, shuffling over to a closet where several shapeless garments were hanging up. "You look like an advertisement for the Salvation Army in those clothes. You'll give my cafe a bad name."

A bad name? I grinned to myself, took the uniform, and went through into the bathroom to put it on. It was an orange polyester minidress with big puffy sleeves and a little white apron. Hopelessly old-fashioned. I bet they hadn't changed the uniforms since the café first opened a zillion years ago. I looked at myself in horror. How could he make me wear polyester! *Maybe one of my first jobs can be to design a new uniform,* I thought.

Mr Garbarini didn't seem to think I looked so dreadful. "That's better," he growled. "You can dump your things in this closet. We keep it locked. Now, the first thing you can do is fill all those condiment bottles. Then, when we get the grill going, I'll show you how to make hamburgers."

"Am I going to be a cook or a waitress?" I asked, trying to sound brisk and efficient.

"Everything," he said. "There's usually only two people working at once, so you'll just have to do whatever needs doing – working the coffee machine, making the hamburgers, cleaning the tables, washing up."

"I see," I said. At least I wouldn't be chained to a hot stove all day. "Okay. Show me where you keep the condiments and I'll get started."

I could see he was already beginning to think better of me. He took me on a rapid tour of the kitchen, which was pretty clean and neat, and got me started pouring ketchup from huge plastic jars into small plastic jars. It was actually kind of fun, trying to guess how much to pour in one go without it slopping over the sides. I had got it down to practised flick of the wrist and was finishing up the last bottle of mustard with no mishaps when I heard the front door rattling, then someone coming in. I glanced up at the clock. It was only ten-thirty. I put on my most efficient voice.

"I'm sorry," I said. "We're still closed. We open at eleven."

Instead of going back out again, the person closed the front door behind him and came across the room towards me. It was another biker, all black leather and space-age helmet again.

"Who the hell are you?" he asked.

I hadn't considered until now that part of the job might be dealing with difficult customers. I had the secure feeling of knowing that Mr Garbarini was in the back somewhere, but all the same, I wasn't too easy as he went over to the counter and calmly took off his helmet.

I recognized him at the same moment he recognized me. My parking-space thief from the day before had returned.

"What are you going here?" he demanded.

"I work here."

"Since when?"

"Since this morning."

He rolled his eyes upwards, sort of like the old man had done. "Oh, no, don't tell me you're the one he hired! I told him he was getting senile ..."

"More to the point," I said, trying to ignore the insult, "is what are *you* doing here? I just said we were still closed, or couldn't you wait for your French fry fix?"

"I happen to run this place," he said, putting his helmet down on the nearest table.

"Oh, sure," I said, grinning at him for the first time.

"You don't believe me?"

"Not unless you've been through some kind of time warp in the past five minutes," I said. "Last time I saw the owner, he was about sixty-five."

"I didn't say I was the owner," he answered. "Hey, Poppa," he called. "Get in here!"

Mr Garbarini poked his head through from the kitchen. "Oh, Joe, it's you. About time you showed up. I got extra work for you today. I want you to show this young lady how we do things round here."

"What did you have to hire her for?" the biker asked, walking over to the counter, his back to me. "I told you I'd find us somebody."

"But when, Joey, when?" the old man asked. "How can I take it easy when I can't leave the place, eh?" He pointed across the room at me. "She came in, she wanted the job, we give her a try. What's wrong with that?"

"Plenty," Joe said, looking back at me as if I were some lower life-form. "Look at her, Poppa. She drives a fancy sports car and she belongs to the country club and she has hysterics when she can't get her own way."

"You know her?" Mr Garbarini demanded, the prawns dancing up and down.

"Enough to know that she won't work out," Joe said, not even looking at me. It was as if I wasn't even a person in his eyes. He gestured with his hands for emphasis. "Why would she want to work here? It's probably some dumb girl's club dare!"

"How do you know I don't need a job just as much as you do?" I interrupted finally.

Joe looked at me as if my opinion didn't matter. "You need a new air filter for your sports car?" he added. "I thought people like you just got new cars when the air filters got dirty."

Mr Garbarini thumped his fist down on the counter, making bottles rattle on the shelves. "She says she needs a job and that's good enough for me!" he said. He leaned over towards me. "You have to forgive my grandson," he said. "He likes to think that he runs this place single-handedly, just because I had a heart attack last fall and the doctors tell me I got to rest. But I'm not dead yet! He should remember that – this is still my cafe and I say what goes until they carry me away. Got that?"

Joe shrugged his shoulders. "Okay, Poppa," he said. "Have it your way."

"I will have it my way and don't you forget it," Mr Garbarini yelled. "Now get dressed and show this young lady where the lettuce and tomatoes are kept. And get the coffee started. We've got customers coming in half an hour."

He stomped back into the kitchen again, leaving Joe and me staring at each other like two boxers who have just climbed into the ring together. I was still feeling hot and uncomfortable after having to listen to them discuss me as if I weren't there. I was also pretty embarrassed about not believing Joe ran the place. It seemed that I'd better say something to break the ice.

"He's your grandfather?" I asked at last.

"That's right."

"And you help him run the place?"

"Most days I run it alone," Joe said. "He hasn't been able to put in a full day's work since his heart attack."

"Do you still go to school?" I asked. Up close, he didn't look much older than I was.

"I go to Harbor High," he said.

"I go to Oakview," I said.

"It figures."

"I might have seen you at a basketball game or something," I suggested. Harbor High was our biggest rival.

"I don't get time for basketball games any more. I have to work," Joe answered. "And we don't have time to stand around talking. This place gets crazy pretty quickly on Saturdays. I'll show you how to do the lettuce and tomatoes. You know how to slice tomatoes?" he asked, stalking ahead of me into the kitchen and yanking open a refrigerator drawer.

"Of course I do," I said. "I'm not quite helpless, you know. I can cook."

He put lettuce and tomatoes out on the counter and handed me a knife. "Somehow I don't think toasting marshmallows at summer camp counts," he said with a smirk, making me wonder whether he was psychic or something.

"I think you're in for a surprise," I said coldly. "I usually manage to do anything I put my mind to."

He lit the gas grill with a loud pop and a spurt of blue flame. "I'll bet you won't last a month," he said, looking over at me with a hint of challenge in his eyes.

"You're on!" I shot back.

Chapter Four

At the end of the day I staggered home, exhausted. I hadn't really done all that much; Mr Garbarini had insisted I watch Joe and learn about everything first. He only gave me tasks when something desperately needed doing. Washing the dishes consisted of loading and unloading an industrial-size dishwasher, and the only physically hard work had been when I had to mop up a few spills. But I wasn't used to being on my feet for hours on end, and my head was throbbing from the loud music; Heartbreak Café patrons tended to prefer heavy metal. My brain was also crammed with everything I had learned that day. I definitely did not want to look like an idiot in front of Mr Garbarini and especially not in front of his grandson, so I had tried to remember every word the first time. I was determined to do the job perfectly, so that they both would have to admit they were wrong about me and that wearing pink designer flats did not necessarily mean a person is a wimp.

The day had been crazy – nonstop traffic from the moment we opened, all the customers wanting instant service, all putting quarters in the jukebox, which kept the place filled with a constant pulsating beat. Joe hardly slowed down for a minute – flipping hamburgers, toasting buns, rushing out with four plates of orders balanced in his arms. I did a lot of lettuce and tomato chopping and cleared away a lot of dirty plates. I was concentrating so hard on trying to remember the correct temperature setting for French fries, the number of pickles on a regular burger, and how many scoops of ice cream went on a Chocolate Madness that I was only dimly aware of the customers. I did notice with surprise, however, that they weren't the bikers and rowdies I had expected. They were just kids. Oh, some were pretty weird-looking, with punk haircuts and blue lips, but mostly they were surfers and beach freaks. No one from my crowd, of course. My friends wouldn't exactly fit in there. But not as bad as I'd expected either.

Around seven o'clock my legs began to sag. "How long is my shift supposed to be?" I asked Joe.

"You had enough?"

"It's just usual to work a set number of hours," I said. "Don't you have an evening shift coming on?"

"What do you think this is, McDonald's?" he asked. "But it's okay. You can go. We'll manage."

I glared at him. "I just wanted to know what to expect," I said coldly.

"I said you can go," he answered.

"I know you did, but you make it sound like you're doing me a special favour." My voice rose over the loud thump of the jukebox. "In normal places they have labour laws, don't they? Time and a half after eight hours, that sort of thing. My father was always taking people to court about stuff like that."

"Your father's a lawyer? It figures."

"He used to be," I said.

"What happened?"

"None of your business," I said. "Should I tell your grandfather I'm going?"

"He's not here. He's already gone," Joe answered. "He's supposed to be resting, not killing himself in a dumb café." "Oh," I said, feeling embarrassed at my outburst. "So you're all alone here, then?"

"Don't worry about it," Joe said. "The evening crowd doesn't order much food. It's mostly coffee and hanging out. Once the sun goes off the beach, it's mostly regulars and I can handle them."

"Well, if you're really sure ... I said, my tired legs sending signals that were conflicting with my conscience.

"Go!" Joe yelled.

"Do you need me tomorrow?"

"If you want to learn enough to be any use to us, you'd better come watch again," Joe said, not even looking at me as he filled two glasses with rootbeer and dropped in big scoops of ice cream.

His tone infuriated me. "In case you didn't notice," I said, "I worked, too."

Joe gave me a quick, appraising look. "Oh, yeah, sure."

"There are plenty of other jobs I could get, you know," I said.

"That's what I've been telling myself. I can see you filing in Daddy's law office or handing out towels at the ladies' spa. What made you apply here?"

"To prove to myself and certain other nameless people that a job like this is a piece of cake for an intelligent, educated, fit person like myself," I said.

He let out a funny little half snort, which was the closest he had come to laughing. "I still give you a month," he said.

"So I only have to show up tomorrow if I want to observe you creating the perfect hamburger, right?" I asked, ignoring his remark. "What a thrill that will be. I can hardly wait."

He picked up the coffee cups and began to walk out of the kitchen. "No, you'd better show up tomorrow," he said, "or else my grandfather will blame me for driving you away."

It was the first hint I had got from Joe that he had any human feelings at all. For the briefest second our eyes met.

"See you tomorrow then," I said.

"Hey, kid," he called over his shoulder. "I guess you didn't do too badly today, considering . . ."

"Considering what?" I demanded.

He tried to conceal a grin. "Considering that the most strenuous thing you've done before is probably lift your pinkie when you drink your tea!"

"Shows how little you know about things," I said hotly. "I have done many things that make this look like a piece of cake."

"Actually walked round the golf course instead of driving the cart?" he asked. He was clearly enjoying himself. He looked so superior, standing there and grinning, that I wanted to throw a plastic ketchup bottle at him and walk out, but that would mean that he had won. He claimed I wouldn't last, and if I walked out he'd be right.

"Bicycled across Europe last summer," I said smoothly. "And back!" Then I did my grand sweep towards the door. "I have to go," I called back. "My boyfriend will be waiting." Then I made my grand exit.

Driving home I ached all over with tiredness. My legs felt like lead, which didn't make driving any easier. *I don't have to go back tomorrow*, I told myself. *I haven't even filled in any forms or anything. I'm not even working there officially. They don't even know my address!*

It was very tempting. I just wouldn't show up the next day. I'd go to the movie theatre or a nice clothes store and get a real job. I wouldn't be likely ever to see Joe or his grandfather again, so it wouldn't matter, would it? Then I told myself, very firmly, that it would matter. Even if I never saw Joe or Mr Garbarini again, I didn't want to give them the satisfaction of being right. *A chimpanzee could handle that job*, I said to myself. I learned almost everything in one day. It didn't take much intelligence to cook hamburgers. I'd bet I could do it better than any of them by the end of the week!

After a soak in the tub, I felt almost human again, although my mother had made the mistake of cooking hamburgers for supper. I told her I was eating out with Grant, which was a lie. We were really going to the movies, but I'd rather have starved than face another hamburger.

Grant arrived at a quarter to eight, looking more strikingly preppie than usual in his pink polo shirt, which accentuated his tan. He had a white cotton sweater draped over his shoulders, not a hair on his sleek, dark head out of place, as always. I had got used to the way he looked, but tonight I couldn't help contrasting his appearance to the torn jeans, denim jackets, and weird T-shirts I'd seen down at the café. *He'd have a fit if he saw them,* I thought, then immediately realized that he'd have a fit if he knew where I was working, period. Grant was a wonderful person, but he did tend to think that the civilized world ended just past the gates to the country club. So did I sometimes.

He escorted me politely to the car and bent to give me a kiss on the forehead before he opened the door for me. "How are you surviving slumming it in the dreaded condos?" he asked, his serious brown eyes looking at me with pity and understanding. I had given him a day-by-day account of the horrors of condo living, emphasizing the lady for ever in curlers who lived next door and the thin walls and the fight the couple in the apartment below us had one night. I guess I had enjoyed making my problems as dramatic as possible, but suddenly I didn't want to talk about it any more. The last thing I needed was pity.

"I'm surviving," I said.

"Look at it this way – it's preparing you for college," Grant said, starting the engine with a fierce vroom, then easing his Alfa Romeo out of the narrow parking lot. "I understand the dorms are very cramped and ugly, even at Harvard. I'm going to have to keep a trailer on campus, just for my clothes." I looked at him and he gave me a little smile. "Well, why not?" he asked, laughing.

He put his foot down on the gas, and the condo project dropped away behind us. Grant was attempting to be cheerful and all I could think of was that I might be stuck in our gross condo instead of a dorm. I swallowed hard and tried to smile back.

"How was your day?" he asked. "You're so quiet."

"My day?" It came out as a squeak. I knew I had to tell him about the Heartbreak some time, but I didn't feel up to telling him right now. I glanced over at him, noticing how confident and relaxed he always looked when he drove. Would he freak out when I told him? Would he feel extra sorry for me or repulsed by the whole idea? I ran through some possible scenes in my mind: Grant begging me to marry him rather than wash dishes versus Grant stopping the car and ordering me to get out and walk all the way home. Neither was something I could handle right at this moment. I decided to put off the inevitable until later. "Pretty boring," I said. "How was yours?"

"Had to caddy for my father this morning," Grant said. "Got some studying done this afternoon for my physics test. Thrilling day, right?"

"Sounds like we both need an exciting movie to liven things up," I suggested.

Grant took me at my word and we went to see the new thriller about a Russian plot to blow up the president. It was the kind of picture where the tension is almost unbearable – lots of shots of fuses slowly burning away and men sitting around a dinner table while a bomb is ticking away in the flower arrangement. I guess it was a pretty good movie, but I couldn't judge because I fell asleep after the first five minutes. I kept jerking awake as my head dropped forward, watching a car chase or a couple of shootings, then falling back to sleep again. Luckily Grant was so absorbed in the movie that he hardly noticed, and when I finally put my head on his shoulder, he just thought I was being affectionate.

The more I thought about telling Grant about my job, the more I decided it would be a bad idea. It wasn't that he was exactly a snob, but I just knew he'd think a rundown café was not the right place for a person like me to be working. I didn't like the idea of lying to him, but I decided I had to break it to him gradually. Luckily he was so involved in so many things, from student government to the tennis team, that we really only saw each other once or twice a week.

I didn't want my friends at school to know about the café either. They were all part of the country club set – where the word *Café* meant a chic little place that served espresso and croissants. The only person I could tell the truth to was Pam Paulson. Pam had been my best friend since kindergarten, and we'd always told each other everything. We were opposites in many ways – I was thin and a little hyper, and she was patient and steady and a little on the heavy side. She was also the person who'd had to put up with my moods since the divorce, and I knew she'd be hurt if I ever lied to her. The other reason I decided to tell Pam was that she did not judge people. If you told her something embarrassing, she never came out and said, "Boy, was that dumb" or "Why on earth did you make a fool of yourself like that?" She just nodded in her quiet, wise way and let you keep on talking. Sometimes I thought that Pam must have been born with an old soul. I'd never seen her do anything really crazy.

On Monday morning she was waiting for me beside my locker.

"Where were you all weekend?" she asked. "I called and called and you were never there."

"I've got a job," I said, opening my locker and stuffing in my books.

"A job? Cool! What is it?"

"You know that little café down at the beach?"

"La Lanterna? They have the greatest chocolate croissants."

"Not that one, the one on the street behind it – the Heartbreak?"

She wrinkled her nose. Pam is sort of an extra-neat, fastidious type person, in direct contrast to me – I like to look nice, but am, by nature, a slob.

"The Heartbreak?" she asked.

"You know the one I'm talking about?"

"Of course I do," she said. She still looked shocked, but being Pam, she didn't say anything.

"How is it?" she asked politely as I collected my books for first period.

"Not too bad, although some pretty weird types seem to hang out there. I spent most of the time this weekend just observing, but I understand the serious work starts tonight."

"You're working there every day?" She couldn't disguise her concern this time. "What about homework?"

"Not every day," I said. "We didn't exactly discuss a schedule yet. Things are a little disorganized down there, to say the least, but I couldn't handle it full-time. I don't know how this guy Joe does it, but then I don't suppose his schoolwork goes much beyond auto shop," I added with a grin.

We began to walk down the hall, our feet making neat tapping sounds on the linoleum.

"Why, Debbie?" Pam asked, looking at me.

"Why'm I working? Because I have to pay my own car expenses now," I said. "My mother's going back to school and we're poor. Lots of poor kids have to work."

Pam winced. "Why the Heartbreak, I meant. What do your parents think about it?"

"My mother doesn't care at all," I said. "She's totally wrapped up in her college courses."

"I'm sure that's not true," Pam insisted. "You know she cares about you. Whose mother always drove to school when she forgot her lunch? Whose mother sat up all night sewing a costume when you forgot to mention you were a pilgrim in a play?"

"That was then," I said. "She seems to have forgotten about being a mother these days."

"She's just got a lot on her mind right now," Pam said quietly. "It's not easy for her adjusting to a new life style."

"I think she's adjusting very easily," I said coldly. "She's totally into being a college student. She acted horrified for about two seconds when I told her about the café, mumbled something about finding me a real job, then went back to her college catalogues."

"And your dad?" Pam asked quietly.

I pushed back my hair. "I haven't told him yet. I've hardly seen him since he moved out. I guess he's very busy with finding a place to live and starting to write and all that stuff. He hasn't stopped by the condo since that night he took me out to dinner, and I don't like to call him while he's staying with someone else. But he'd probably think it was pretty funny if he knew."

Pam looked at me steadily. "Are you maybe trying to get back at your parents for putting you through all this?"

"Of course not," I answered, a little too forcefully. "Why would I want to do that? It's a job. One job's pretty much the same as any other." I firmly shut out the nagging little voice whispering to me that Pam was probably right, that maybe getting back at my parents, shocking them back to sanity, had been one of the things that made me take this job. Why else would I have taken it? I still wasn't sure myself, but I had the feeling that nobody with any sense would choose to wash dishes in a crummy café if they could work anywhere else. I glanced over at Pam. Her face was tight with concern. "It's not as bad as you think," I said, my voice echoing, bright and normal down the empty hallway. Right now I didn't think I could handle Pam's feeling sorry for me either. A month earlier, I'd been a person that other people admired or envied. I'd always been a good student, always been involved in lots of school activities, and for the past year I'd had one of the most desirable boyfriends at Oakview. Pity was something new to me, and I didn't like it. "In fact, it's kind of fun," I went on quickly. "I thought it would be a real sleazy place, but it's not. Just a lot of kids hanging out after the beach. You have to drop by and see it some time. You might get a laugh! Also, I understand their Chocolate Madness is sinful."

"Chocolate Madness?" Pam asked. She loves anything fattening. You'd probably guess that from looking at her – she's always trying some new diet, but never stays on it for long.

"Chocolate Madness," I said. "It happens that I now know exactly how to make one: first you take a chocolate brownie – a very good chocolate brownie, baked by some Italian bakers who are relatives of Mr Garbarini – then you put two scoops of chocolate ice cream on top, pour chocolate syrup over that, whipped cream over the chocolate syrup, and top it all off with chopped nuts."

"Sounds like my kind of dessert," Pam said. "I think I'll take you up on your offer. Do friends of staff get free samples?"

"I don't know," I said. "I haven't had time to eat anything while I'm there yet, but I can't see Joe letting me hand out favours. He'd think my friends could afford to pay for their Chocolate Madnesses!"

"Joe's the boss?"

"He likes to think he is," I said. "He's Mr Garbarini's grandson, but Mr Garbarini had a heart attack and can't work much, so Joe almost runs the place. He's a senior at Harbor High, and he has an ego about the size of Texas."

"I take it you don't exactly like him," Pam said.

"He's just got such a chip on his shoulder about being working class and me being a rich princess," I said. "He's just waiting for me to make a mistake so he can prove he's right."

"Sounds like a real pain," Pam said. "Cute or no?"

"Good looking," I said, "which is not the same as cute. Cute implies a certain degree of niceness. Bambi was cute."

Pam laughed. "At least he doesn't have spindly legs and a large brown nose."

"No, there's nothing spindly or delicate about Joe," I said.

"He's sort of rugged-looking – lots of black curly hair and muscle shirts, like those guys who sit on rocks in the cigarette ads."

"Doesn't sound too bad at all," Pam said. "I'll have to come down and see for myself. Does he have a girlfriend?"

"I don't know," I said. "He certainly flirts enough – with every girl in the place."

"Including you?"

"Not including me."

"Aha," Pam said with a little smile. "That might be it."

"Be what?" I demanded, pausing to glare at her.

"The cause behind all the animosity," she said, still smiling.

"What are you talking about?"

"Elementary, my dear Watson," she said. "Don't forget I'm taking psych this year . . . You're mad because an obviously sexy guy is ignoring you!"

"That's ridiculous and totally untrue," I said. "The very last thing in the world I would want is to have a classless lout like Joe Garbarini interested in me."

I could hear her laughing as I swivelled and stalked into my chemistry lab.

Chapter Five

All weekend the Heartbreak had been a confusing jumble of cooking, serving, cleaning, and people coming and going. On the slower weekday shifts, however, I had a little more time to breathe between carrying out dirty dishes and slicing tomatoes. I noticed that there was a group of regulars who seemed to use the Heartbreak as a sort of second home. I was horrified at first. These kids had nothing better to do with their lives than sit around in a café. Every evening! Didn't they have any homework? Didn't they have any other friends? What about their parents, their families? But it just seemed like this was their home, like they didn't have anywhere to go that was better.

The first regular I came face to face with was Ashley. I had shown up for work on Monday and was relieved to find only Mr Garbarini there.

"Think you've got the hang of things?" he asked. "Can I let you loose on my customers without you spilling stuff all over them?"

I assured him I would be just fine. I'd learned everything over the weekend.

He snorted. "That's good, because Joe needed a day off," he said.

Now was my chance to show what a quick learner I was. I imagined Joe's face when he came back to work the next day and his grandfather told him how I'd handled everything single-handedly.

I sliced up vegetables, stocked the big coffee pot, and then went out to the big freezer on the back porch to get ice cream to stock the inside freezer.

The back porch had an open-weave concrete wall around it, letting in the light and air, but protecting it from the worst of the weather and also keeping the contents reasonably hidden. The garbage cans were kept back there, and there was an extra industrial sink as well as the spare freezer. I was bending down, trying to read the iced-over labels on the big, five-gallon ice cream cartons, when someone whispered to me through the concrete screen.

"Hi there, honey," breathed a very seductive girl's voice. She was just a few inches from my head, on the other side of the screen. "Did you miss me all weekend? I sure missed you. Do you want to know how much I missed you? I was pining for you every single minute ..."

I straightened up from my crouching position, not knowing exactly what to say or do. I only hoped the person thought I was someone else.

"Don't get mad at me, okay?" the breathy voice continued. It was very close to the way Marilyn Monroe's voice sounded in all those old movies. "I hate it when you get mad at me. I can't help loving you, you know that. And one day you're going to come round and see that I'm the right girl for you."

I thought I'd better put an end to this. I was about to creep back into the kitchen, so that the unknown girl would never know she'd been talking to me, but she found a gap in the concrete wall and peered through. I found myself inches from a doll face – so expertly made up that it was hard to tell exactly what the person looked like underneath. Her eyes were outlined and mascaraed to make them look as big as a doll's. They opened even wider in disbelief.

"You're not Joe!" she shrieked.

"Sorry!" I mumbled.

"Where's Joe?" she demanded, as if I were responsible for hiding him.

"He's taking the day off."

She let out a huge wail. "Oh, no, I came all the way down here for nothing. I borrowed my mom's car, and she's going to kill me, and all for nothing! Oh, I could just kill myself right now!"

And people had told me I tended to be overly dramatic! "Joe will be here again tomorrow," I said. "I could tell him you came by."

Her eyes flew open again, so instantly that I began to wonder if she wasn't really a life-size Barbie and someone was flicking a switch—"Get new super-sized surprised Barbie! It's easy to make her act surprised when you tell her things – just push this button!" I started to giggle. The girl obviously didn't think anything was funny. She directed those oversized eyes at me and seemed to take me in for the first time.

"Who are you, anyway?" she asked. "And what are you doing hiding out back here?"

"I'm Debbie. I work here now and I wasn't hiding, I was transferring these ice cream cartons inside," I said.

She continued to stare at me as if she were wishing I would go away. "You work here now?" she asked.

"That's right."

"Oh, no!" Another wail.

It was unnerving to have those disembodied eyes staring at me without blinking through the hole in the concrete. I took a step back towards the door.

"Does Joe know you're working here?" she asked.

"Yes."

"Oh, rats," she said strongly. "Now that's another girl. It's not fair."

I got her meaning. "I wouldn't worry about me," I said. "I'm not entering the Joe Garbarini Sweepstakes. He's all yours as far as I'm concerned.

"I wish," she said. "Sometimes I think he'll never notice me, never ever." She poked her face further into the hole, craning her neck to look round as if she still wasn't quite convinced Joe wasn't hiding in a corner or standing just inside the kitchen, and I was just keeping her away from him. "What do you think?" she asked.

I didn't know what to say. A girl I met two seconds ago was now asking me to play Dear Abby. I was about to answer that from what I had seen, Joe wasn't worth a broken heart and that boys with big egos are not great to date, but her expression was so expectant, trusting.

I grinned encouragingly. "The way he flirts, I would think he'll run out of other girls eventually," I said. "Then you'll get your chance."

"You really think so?" she asked.

"I don't know for sure," I said. "I just got here. I don't know Joe or you yet."

"I'm Ashley," she said. "Didn't he tell you about me yet? Didn't he ask where I was all weekend?"

"I was too busy learning what to do," I answered tactfully. "I didn't have time to talk." I picked up a tub of chocolate ice cream. "I really have to get a move on," I said. "I have a million things to do."

Her eyes fastened on the chocolate ice cream. "I think I'll just pop inside and eat my sorrows away," she said. "I'm on this new diet."

"I don't think we serve too much diet food – from what I've seen of the menu, anyway," I said cautiously, wondering how fat the body was that went with the face.

"I'm going to have the Chocolate Madness," she said excitedly. "I always have that."

"On a diet?" I asked.

"Oh, I'm on the chocolate lover's diet," she said happily. "I read all about it in the National Enquirer last week. Did you know that scientists have actually proven that chocolate melts away calories? Isn't that terrific? Of course, I can't eat too much or my face breaks out, but I'm sure willing to give it a try. See you inside, okay?" The face disappeared and I was left feeling like I was back in my Alice in Wonderland mode. When I finally met all of Ashley, she was not fat at all; in fact, she was super-skinny, dressed in a low-cut sweater and pants so tight that I expected to hear them rip when she sat down.

"I'd better only have one scoop on the Chocolate Madness," she said. "Bikini season starts next month and I really don't want to go on the grapefruit and garlic diet again. Have you heard of that one? You should try it some time." I couldn't tell from the way she looked at me whether she thought I needed it or not. She had been looking at me suspiciously since she came into the café. I guess she was embarrassed about the things she'd said to me outside. Out there, it had been like talking in a confessional to a half-seen person. Now that she saw me in the flesh, she probably regretted all the things she'd said.

"Grapefruit and garlic?" I replied. "You eat them together?"

Her face lit up. "I read about it last year," she said. "Did you know that scientists have proven that grapefruit and garlic actually destroy fat cells?"

"Amazing," I said, knowing she expected me to be impressed.

She nodded, as if she was proud of having said something profound. "It works real well," she added, "because I hate grapefruit and garlic so much that I don't eat anything for a week." She stared at me appraisingly. "Do you have a boyfriend?"

I nodded. Ashley smiled. "That's good," she said, which made me think that the suspicious looks I had been getting had more to do with Joe than with anything she had told me. So I went on to describe in detail how close Grant and I were and how long we had been going together. After that I think she looked a little happier.

I'm learning how to say the right thing to customers, I thought.

It wasn't long after meeting Ashley that I met another regular, Howard. I had noticed him over the weekend, because he was reading a Batman comic, and when I brought him a banana split he hadn't even looked up from the comic, as if it was the most exciting thing in the world. On Monday afternoon, however, he came over especially to talk to me. I was in the kitchen, spreading mayonnaise on buns while Mr Garbarini cooked patties, and I didn't know anyone was watching me until I looked up to see Howard leaning in over the counter. He looked like an ad for *Revenge of the Nerds:* runtish in size, hair that spiked in all the wrong directions, glasses that kept sliding to the end of his nose, and a sweater with a picture of a stag knitted into it in brown and purple.

"I'm Howard," he said, smiling at me so intensely that I took a step back. "I think you do that very well," he added.

"I'm only spreading mayonnaise," I said cautiously.

"Yes, but you're doing it very well, very evenly over the whole bun. I like my mayonnaise spread evenly," he said. His voice was even squeaky. "You're new here, right?"

"Right."

"I saw you yesterday," he said, "but it's too busy to talk on weekends. I don't usually come on weekends because I don't like crowds. Are you one of Joe's girls?"

I was torn between telling him I was Joe's girl, which would keep him from coming on to me, and denying that I was Joe's girl because I didn't want anybody to think that. I chose the latter because I didn't want any wrong ideas to get back to Joe. Knowing his ego, he'd think that I had a secret crush on him.

"No," I said firmly. "I'm not Joe's girl. I have a steady boyfriend. We've been going together for over a year now."

Howard nodded, digesting this. "Do you like movies?" he asked.

"Sure."

"I love movies," he said. "I adore them. I live for them. To me movies are more real than life. Life is very unreal, don't you think?"

"Right now it is," I said, glancing around at Mr Garbarini and hoping that he'd yell that the patties were waiting and I'd better hurry up.

Howard leaned even further into the kitchen, making me concerned that he'd wind up falling head first on to one of my mayonnaised buns. His face was radish coloured with the effort. "Have you been to the movies recently?" he asked.

"My boyfriend and I went on Saturday," I answered, stressing the word *boyfriend*.

Howard stared at me excitedly. "Have you seen *Revenge of the Swamp Beast* yet?" he asked.

"Er, no. Not yet."

"You must see it," he said forcefully. "It is fantastic. The special effects – when he comes out of the swamp with this girl's leg in his mouth – it's so real. Man, you'd think that was a real leg the way the arteries are spurting blood."

"Er, I think I'd better take these orders through," I said, almost snatching the patties from Mr Garbarini.

"Of course," Howard continued, following me across the café, "it would be hard to improve on the first in the trilogy, *Curse of the Swamp Beast*. You saw that, didn't you?"

"Er, no, I think I must have been out of town when that was showing."

"A classic!" he cried, making the guy I'd just delivered a hamburger to almost miss the plate with his ketchup. "What a classic. The maiden-devouring scenes in that are the best ever."

I could sense that the two diners were about to be treated to a blow-by-blow description of maidens being digested, so I grabbed Howard by the arm and steered him away from their table. "I'll make a note to see it on the Movie Channel," I said.

"Maybe we can get some people together, make a party of it," Howard said excitedly. "It will have to be at your place, though. We don't get the Movie Channel. My old man objects to spending money on that sort of thing."

I tried not to shudder as I pictured a room full of Howards, all crammed into our little condo living room, all eating popcorn like crazy as the Swamp Beast crunched his way through an entire cheerleading squad.

"We'll talk about it later, Howard, all right?" I said. "Right now I'm way behind with my work and Mr Garbarini will start yelling at me."

At that moment I was actually praying that Mr Garbarini would start yelling. I wanted him to tell me to get into the kitchen and not come out until I'd cleaned the entire French fryer or unloaded the dishwasher. He didn't yell, but I walked calmly into the kitchen.

"I thought I'd clean the French fryer while we have a break in customers," I said, beginning to polish it furiously.

"It is clean. It was cleaned Saturday," he growled. "Why don't you take a break? Fix yourself some food?"

"But it's not shining," I insisted. "I can't sit down to eat until it shines." I began to polish more furiously at the stainless steel. Mr Garbarini shook his head. "You're going to give my grandson a guilt complex if you start working too hard," he said.

I grinned to myself as I cleaned, imagining Joe's face when his grandfather said, "How come you can't get this thing to shine the way Debbie can? Maybe she can teach you what hard work really is?" Then I'd look angelic and mysterious and say nothing.

Actually, I was not finding the job was hard work. Monday evening was very quiet after the weekend, and Mr Garbarini was handling all the cooking, so I had plenty of time to get things cleared away in between customers.

Piece of cake, I thought to myself. *I might even be able to bring down my homework and do it in quiet periods.*

I drove home that night feeling pretty confident. I'd worked a whole shift, almost unsupervised, and I hadn't done anything dumb. When I saw Joe again, he'd be amazed that I had learned everything so quickly. That would show him that people with superior intellect could tackle anything they put their minds to!

I arrived home at ten o'clock and was met by my anxious mother.

"Where on earth have you been?" she demanded even before I'd closed the door.

"I told you," I said quietly. "I had to work."

"Until ten o'clock?"

"The café is open until midnight. Mr Garbarini let me go early."

She frowned at me. She looked as if she was trying to read my thoughts. "You've really been working at that café?" she asked.

I laughed. "You still don't believe me, do you? You think I'm making it all up and I really spent the evening at Pam's."

"Oh, no, I know you weren't at Pam's," she said. "I called there and she said she thought you were working."

"So there you are," I said.

She perched herself cautiously on the edge of the sofa. "You're really working at that place?" she asked. "Until ten o'clock at night?"

"That's right."

"Isn't that a little ... unwise, Deborah?" she asked. My parents had never come right out and forbidden me to do things. They had always adopted the approach of trying to make me see the sense in what they were saying. They had suggested it might be unwise to spend the weekend alone up at Grant's family's cabin at the lake, and unwise to go to a football team party where they knew there would be a keg of beer, and unwise to hang out with a girl who had a bad reputation. Each of these times in the past, I had listened to them – a dutiful daughter wanting to please her concerned parents. I did not go to the lake with Grant, nor to the party with the keg, and I stopped being friends with the wrong sort of girl. But this time unwise didn't seem to matter any more. I might have come right back and told her that it didn't seem particularly wise to me to give up a career as a lawyer and start writing screenplays in a writers' commune on the beach, or to sell a beautiful house and move into a Sleazeville condo, and go back to school at age thirty-nine to make up for missed literature and art. In fact, of the three people in our former family unit, it seemed that right now, I was the only one showing any wisdom at all. I needed to pay my car expenses, and I'd got myself a job.

"What's unwise about it?" I answered.

I could sense her discomfort. She hated talking about sensitive matters; in fact, she and my father were real prudes when it came to discussing sex or any delicate topic. "Think about it, Deborah," she said shortly. "A young girl, walking alone to a car in a darkened parking lot ... easy prey for the sort of people who'd be in your café."

I laughed at this. "Mom. It's not a darkened parking lot – I park right beside the building, okay? And there was nobody in the café who was the least bit dangerous," I said.

"Even so," she said, still not used to a daughter who was determined to get her own way and didn't take advice. "Even so, there is a question of homework. I know how much homework you have. You'll hardly have time to do it if you don't come home until ten o'clock, will you?"

"You're the one who told me to get a job, remember?" I asked.

"I told you that it was up to you, and that if you wanted to keep the car—"

"And I do, so I have to work," I said.

"But not so much," she said. I could tell she felt guilty. "All weekend and now all week? You'll have a breakdown if you try to do too much."

I was torn between reassuring her that I did not intend to work seven days a week and wanting to make her feel even more guilty and ashamed. It was late at night and I was tired. The guilt won. "I can hardly pay for car insurance if I only put in a couple of hours a week, can I?" I asked. "I'm only getting four fifty an hour."

She sighed, such a deep, hopeless sigh that I instantly felt bad.

"I'll leave enough time for homework, Mom," I said. "I've only been there so much because they wanted to train me. Now I'm trained and I can work normal shifts ... and if every night is as quiet as tonight, I'll even have time to study in between customers."

She slid from the sofa and came over to me, putting her hands on both my shoulders. "If you really insist on getting a job, then let's get you a proper one, darling," she said. "I really don't like the thought of you working in a place like that."

I wanted to say that I wasn't exactly wild over working in a place like the Heartbreak either and that I still spent half my time thinking I should have my head examined. But I didn't. I had found the job without any help. It was *my* job, my own world that nobody else in my life knew anything about, and as such, it was my position of power in a world that was getting wackier by the minute. I had heard what my mother said about getting me a proper job and didn't need to hear more. If I had to work, nobody else was going to choose my job for me!

"It's not too bad at all," I said hurriedly. "It only looked worse to begin with. It's a pretty ordinary café."

Mom wrinkled her nose as if there was a bad smell under it. "But waitressing. It's hardly what I'd have expected my daughter to do. We'll talk to your father about it. Surely with his connections and mine, we can find you something that will give you a little spending money and not be too demanding, but something where you are mixing with our kind of people."

"Mom, don't be such a snob!" I interrupted.

She dropped her hands from my shoulders. "Who's talking about being a snob?" she asked in a clipped voice that showed she was angry. "I'm not the one who sneaks out of the condo via the garbage yard, in case anyone might drive by and see her. I'm not the one who refuses to use the courts or the pool. I'm also not the one who has to go to Harvard or Brown." She suddenly switched tracks completely. "You should see the courses they are offering at Shoreline." She ran across the room and came back with a catalogue. "How does this sound for a course load: Intro to Western Civilization, History of Art, Great Operas Workshop, and Italian 102?"

I stared at her in horror. "Sounds great if you never plan to get a job," I said. "I mean, wouldn't typing and bookkeeping be a little more sensible for you right now?"

"I'm trying to forget about sensible," she said. "Remember – I was sensible for thirty-nine years and look where it got me."

"You produced me," I said, feeling as if this was a personal insult in some way. "I turned out pretty well, didn't I? Straight A student, lead in the play, tennis team, debating team. Seems like you should be satisfied with me.

She nodded. "Oh, I am, dear. But now I want to be satisfied with me, too. If I'm finally taking the plunge and going back to school, why waste time on dreary courses when I could be plunging into the heart of culture? I understand that I have to do some horrible maths courses at some stage, which I'd better get over right away so that you're still around to help me with them, but apart from that, I plan to grow, to spread my wings."

"Great," I muttered, "I've got a mother who's turned into an albatross."

She laughed and ruffled the back of my hair. "You'll be surprised," she said. "Your father thinks he's the only one who has been set free to find himself."

"You're right," I said, more to myself than to her. "I'm constantly surprised. Every minute of every day. In fact, life's just one long surprise right now. I might even be turning into a new life-size surprised Barbie, too. Push the button and my eyes open very wide. See?"

"What are you talking about?" my mother asked, laughing nervously.

"Nothing," I said. "Just cracking up, I guess. Forget about it. Forget I exist."

I began to walk down the hall to my room.

"You see, I told you that ten o'clock was too late to be working," I heard her voice floating behind me down the hall. "You're overtired, that's all."

Overtired, I like that, I muttered to myself as I sat on my bed and kicked one shoe off. *She doesn't know or care what's going on inside my head. She's so wrapped up in her crummy college that she's almost forgotten she's got a child to take care of.* I kicked off the other shoe and lay back among my stuffed animals, letting my giraffe's neck fall across my face. *What's happening to everyone?* I asked the giraffe, who nodded his furry neck wisely. *My parents both seem happy that they've split up. They're not supposed to be happy ... everyone is spreading their wings except me, and I'm just scared silly that they'll all fly away and I'll be left completely alone.*

I wrapped my arms fiercely round the giraffe and hugged him to me. I was dozing off to sleep when I remembered I wasn't even undressed and sat up again. I was glad that I did, because at that moment my mom stuck her head round the door.

"Here," she said. "I made you some hot chocolate.

We'll have to talk about a sensible work schedule for you in the morning. I don't want you exhausting yourself. You'll get sick."

"Thanks," I said, taking the chocolate, "but you don't have to worry about me. I've got this job licked already."

Chapter Six

Everything had gone so smoothly on Monday evening that I was determined to show Joe Garbarini how well I had mastered the job in such a short time. I pictured myself sweeping out of the kitchen with ten orders balanced in my arms, looking back at Joe, and saying, "Why don't you take a break for a while? There doesn't seem to be too much for you to do right now." I grinned to myself all the way down the canyon. This job could turn out to be as stimulating as a tennis game. All through school I kept coming up with possible put-downs to be stored for future use.

What I had not realized, of course, was that Monday was the slowest night at the café. Nobody went to the beach on Mondays, especially not on cloudy Mondays, which yesterday had been. Mr Garbarini was not there, and Joe was already vacuuming the floor when I arrived. I started off my Tuesday shift as a model of efficiency. I had all the condiment bottles filled before Joe could tell me to. I had the sodas stocked and the coffee pots going.

"How did you get along last night without me?" Joe asked as I walked past him with a big box of napkins to refill the holders.

This was a golden opportunity for one of my put-downs. "Oh, weren't you here last night?" I asked sweetly. "I didn't notice."

"You can't have done too badly," he said, "because I didn't see very many broken plates in the garbage can. But then, nobody comes here on Mondays, do they?"

"I met the girl with the crush on you," I mentioned as I stacked napkins.

"Which one?" he asked. Boy, how conceited can you be!

"Is there more than one girl in this state with defective vision?" I asked.

"Is there what?"

"More than one girl who needs glasses?" I asked triumphantly. Really, everything was going perfectly so far.

He gave me an appraising look. "Let me tell you something," he said. "Maybe you're the one with defective vision, because all the other girls seem to like what they see – and they like what they get, too. But then you wouldn't know about romance, would you? I'll bet your boyfriend, Mr Future Lawyer, has to ask permission to hold your hand."

"Mr Future Lawyer also happens to be Mr All-Star Quarterback," I said, "and there is nothing wimpish about him. He also runs a five-minute mile, plays a mean game of tennis, and maintains an A average."

"Well, pardon me," Joe said. "I'll just call him Mr Perfection from now on." He began taking frozen patties out of the freezer and separating them, banging them down hard on the counter. "Of course, all that stuff is just play, isn't it?" he asked. "I mean, school sports and things – they don't prepare you for the real world."

"From what I've seen of the real world, I don't want to be prepared for it," I said. "There, the napkins are finished. What do you want me to do now?"

"Start heating up the grill," he said. "You get to cook tonight."

"Fine," I said. I put on the little cooking cap and picked up a spatula, ready to cook speedily and efficiently. Customers started arriving all at the same time. Joe took orders.

"Two burgers, one quarter-pounder no onions on a sesame

bun," he yelled through the hatch. I took out two of the small patties and one of the large ones. The grill was a long smooth surface with a little trough at one end to catch the extra fat. I scooped some fat from the trough and spread it over the grill's surface, as I had seen Joe do. Then I put the large patty on the grill. It spat at me as cold met hot, making me take a step back, out of reach of the patty, which slid the full length of the grill, went flying out over the grease tray, and landed on the floor. I glanced around to see if Joe could see, then picked it up hurriedly and washed it off under the faucet. This time it spat even more, but I was prepared and prevented the burger from escaping with my spatula. I even got the two little burgers started. Then I remembered about the buns. While I was getting those from the tray, one of the burgers went for a little walk and slid silently on to the floor. I was just in time to catch its brother before he could join it. I realized that the grill must be tilted slightly to drain off excess grease, but I could hardly stand there, holding all the burgers in place, could I?

"How are those orders coming?" Joe called through the hatch.

"Fine. Almost ready," I called back.

"Great. And bring me out a couple of orders of fries at the same time, will you?" he shouted.

Fries! I checked the heat on the French fryer and shoved in a basket of fries. They were sizzling away nicely when I smelled burning and noticed one of the buns about to go up in flames. By the time I'd found another one and hidden my evidence under a lot of lettuce leaves in the garbage can, the hamburgers needed turning. I slid the spatula under it and flipped, the way Joe had done. It was lighter than I expected. The hamburger sailed into the air and disappeared. I searched desperately. It couldn't just have vanished! I had just discovered it, lying at the bottom of a bowl of water I was washing the lettuce in, when Joe actually put his head through the hatch.

"How's everything coming along?" he asked.

"Oh, just swimmingly," I said, not daring to look at him in case I burst out laughing.

"Then speed it up, will you – oh, and watch that bun. You're about to burn it."

I grabbed at the bun. "I'll be right out," I said.

As soon as I saw him walk away, I fished the burger out of the water, dried it off with a paper towel, and shoved it back on the griddle. I didn't attempt to flip the other two, turning them very carefully with a fork this time, and I actually managed to get three pretty normal looking orders ready. I was just congratulating myself when Joe stuck his head through again.

"All ready," I said smoothly.

"That's good because I need two more burgers with fries, one no pickle, and a grilled cheese," he said, taking the plates from me and disappearing again. This time I held on to the burgers so they couldn't sneak away from me. I got the fries going and put the buns on to brown. In fact I would have served a perfect order if Joe hadn't yelled the next order through before I was done. "Two quarter-pounders to go and make it snappy!" he shouted.

By the time I'd separated two quarter-pounder hamburger patties, my buns were all distinctly charred at the edges. I shoved the burgers on anyway and put an extra lot of mayonnaise and onions to disguise the taste. The temperature in the kitchen was beginning to heat up, and I could feel my polyester uniform sticking to my back. I rescued the fries just before they, too, were cremated and thankfully shoved the orders on the counter.

Joe showed up almost immediately. "I'd better take over here," he said. "You're taking too long."

"It's the first time I've done it," I said. "I thought I was doing pretty well."

"There have been a couple of complaints," he added. "One guy said his burger tasted funny, and someone else complained his bun was burned." He took the spatula from me and pushed me aside. "Go take orders," he said. "And you'd better use the pad. You're not used to taking orders in your head yet."

"If you insist," I said frostily.

I was glad to get out of the heat of that kitchen, and I walked into the main café in my most efficient waitress manner.

"Miss, we're ready to order," somebody called from the corner booth.

I stepped up efficiently. "What can I get you?" I asked, my trusty pen at the ready.

There were four boys at the table, all about my age. They reeled off their orders: double cheeseburger, large Coke, two hamburgers, no tomatoes, large fries, small 7-Up, large hamburger, two brownies, hot chocolate with whipped cream . . . I heard them all clearly and made neat little notes to myself as they spoke. But by the time I had crossed the room to the counter, those neat little notes didn't make a bit of sense. Was it the large burger that had no tomatoes? Which one was no mayo? I had to go back and ask them, which made them look at each other and grin, as if I were the stupidest girl in the world. I stomped back to the kitchen again and gave my orders before I could forget them. How could Joe remember so easily when I, with my superior brainpower, had the hardest time not mixing them up? When I delivered them, I mixed them all up again, and the boys had a good time making fun of me as they sorted them out.

"He gets the cheeseburger, with the fries, and I wanted the Coke."

"You must be new here," one of them commented, just as Joe came out of the kitchen.

After that table, I was glad to go over to a tall, muscular, sun-tanned guy standing alone beside the counter. He had longish sunbleached hair and was wearing bright surfing shorts, although the weather was pretty cold, and a torn T-shirt. He looked me over and then nodded as if he liked what he saw. "Hi, gorgeous," he said, and flashed me a brilliant smile. "Are you the new waitress?"

I nodded and he beamed. "Great," he said. "Just what this dump needed – a bit of class." I felt myself blushing like an idiot, feeling that everyone in the café must be watching me.

"I'm Art," he said, resting his elbow easily on the counter so that he was leaning very close to me, "and you are ...?"

"Debbie," I said, trying to step backwards but finding myself trapped.

"Debbie," he said as if it were the most wonderful name in the world instead of being pretty ordinary. "How come I haven't seen you before? Did you just move here?"

"Actually, I've lived here most of my life," I said, "I just don't come down to the beach too much."

He looked as if I'd said I never washed. "You don't come down to the beach?" he asked. "Man, I'd die if I didn't come down here every day. If they took away my surfboard, I swear I'd just shrivel up and die. Do you like to surf?"

"I never tried it, except for body surfing," I said.

He leaned even closer. "You've got to let me teach you when the water gets warmer," he said. "It will be real fun, just you and me in that big ocean ..."

I realized how this scene would look if Joe stuck his head through from the kitchen, so I put on my efficient voice again.

"Did you want to order something, because if not, I've got a lot of work I should be doing."

"Just a large Coke to go," he said. "I want to go out one more time before it gets dark."

I poured him the Coke. "A dollar fifty," I said.

He looked at me tenderly. "You can put that on my tab," he said.

"Your what?"

"I only pay once a month. Didn't they tell you that?" he asked. "The regulars, we only pay once a month. Makes it easier and we don't have to carry cash when we're surfing."

"Oh, uh, okay," I said hesitantly.

"Go write it down," Art said and waved as he walked towards the door.

I picked up a pencil and looked round to see what I should write it on. Joe came through just then with two cups of coffee.

"What are you looking for?" he asked.

"Art's tab."

"Art's *what?*"

"His tab. He told me he only pays once a month, and that I should write it on his tab."

Joe looked at me with utter disbelief. "Were you born yesterday?" he asked. "How could you fall for that line?"

"You mean he doesn't have a tab? He doesn't pay once a month?" I asked, conscious that the people at the nearest tables were all listening.

"Do you really think we'd let somebody pay once a month?" Joe asked. He shook his head. "He can always use those big blue eyes to get round any girl. You fell for it just like the rest."

"How was I supposed to know?" I demanded. "I'll just ask him for the money the next time he comes in."

"Fat chance," Joe said. "You're going to have to wise up to all the excuses. Half our customers don't want to pay, and they'll come out with some real good stories to get out of it, right, guys?"

He turned to the kids at the nearest table. "Right!" they yelled back, laughing. "Remember when Ashley was helping out for the week and Art told her a shark had eaten his wallet?"

I noticed that Ashley was part of the group at the table. She flushed bright red. "I don't see what was so unbelievable about that," she said. "I read in the paper once that they cut a shark open and they found a complete refrigerator inside it. And do you know what? The sodas were still cold!"

"I'd sooner believe about the refrigerator than Art's story," Joe said.

"He still claims that one was true," one of the girls commented.

"I wouldn't believe anything Art told me," another girl said, popping a French fry into her mouth.

"Yeah, well this young lady's led a sheltered life," Joe said, indicating me with a big grin on his face. "She's just been let out of the convent."

All eyes turned to me. "Is that really true? You were a nun?" Ashley asked, staring at me wide-eyed.

"Joe is just trying to get at me," I said. "I'm a perfectly ordinary person."

"From the country club, with the white convertible and a lawyer daddy," Joe added. "Very ordinary."

"No kidding," one of the boys said, looking at me as if I might be a huge joke. "Is it true they serve caviar burgers at that country club?"

"So what are you doing here?" another boy joined in. "Are you doing a term paper on what the real world is like?"

"Strangely enough," I said, trying to keep my face calm, "I'm here because I need the money."

That produced a good laugh. "What happened? Mommie and Daddy won't cough up for Europe again this year? Or maybe you lost your diamond tennis bracelet and you're afraid to tell your folks! Or you want to give your boyfriend a car for his birthday so that you can have his and hers matching convertibles?"

"You all think you're so smart!" I blurted out, "but there's a lot

you don't know. You think you're the only ones who've got problems? Maybe you should wise up and find out how the other half
lives!" Then I strode back to the kitchen. I could hear the conversation about me continuing and Joe's voice, louder than the rest,
saying, "Don't look at me, she wasn't my idea! Don't think I enjoy
working with someone who walks round with her nose two
yards in the air. Can't see her being any use at all – but Poppa
took a liking to her for some reason and he does still own the
place."

"Looks like you're stuck with her, Joe," a girl teased.

"Not necessarily," Joe's voice came back. Then he said something to them I didn't catch, which was followed by loud
laughter.

Chapter Seven

By the end of the week, things had not improved that much. I still could not get orders straight, and I still couldn't cook hamburgers and buns at the same time without burning the buns – and I was getting more and more mad about it daily! I guess I have always been the kind of person who likes to do things well. That comes with being an only child: you like to succeed, or you hate to fail. I always used to lie awake at summer camp, dreaming up ways to win on the obstacle course, and I was devastated when I got a C on a driver's ed test, even though the course was only pass/fail. So it really bugged me that I couldn't remember orders or cook hamburgers well. Until this moment, I had seriously believed that anyone with brains and a good education could do anything they set their minds to. So how was it possible that someone like Joe Garbarini, someone who made fun of education, who probably couldn't count to ten except on his fingers, could remember ten orders without screwing them up, and cook hamburgers, buns, and fries without burning any of them, when I couldn't?

The worst part was that he always seemed to be around when I made my biggest bloopers: like the time I got a little cocky and tossed a hamburger up on to the window ledge. Of course Joe had to be standing right behind me, and of course he had to say, "Trying to ripen it in the sun?" with a big stupid grin on his face. He was also standing right behind me when this serious-faced kid stepped up to the counter.

"A Momma, Poppa, and Baby to go," he said earnestly.

"Excuse me?" I asked. I didn't think I'd heard right.

"I said a Momma, Poppa, and Baby to go," the boy repeated. He looked so serious that I began to suspect that someone was putting me on again.

"Momma, Poppa, and Baby to go?" I asked, trying to look very superior. "Who do you think I am – Goldilocks?" The boy flushed scarlet. "I'm only trying to order," he stammered. "You do serve Poppaburgers here, don't you?"

Of course Joe had to step up at the moment. "I'm sorry," he said. "There's been a misunderstanding. The waitress is new here, and we've stopped calling our burgers that. Now, what can I get you?"

As soon as we were through in the kitchen, Joe looked at me coldly. "It's not too smart to try and score points against our customers, you know," he said.

"How was I to know you used to call your burgers dumb things like that!" I snapped. "I thought it was another of your buddies trying to make me look dumb."

The whole episode made me feel angry as well as stupid, and I spent every chemistry class that week thinking up unique ways to blow up, poison, melt, or exterminate Joe Garbarini!

Then, on Monday morning, after a free day Sunday and a good rest, I made a decision. I would go down to the Heartbreak when nobody was there and practise until I could do everything perfectly. I was not going to let Joe get the better of me. By the end of the month I would not only not have quit – I would be the star hamburger flipper! After school I drove straight down to the café.

"I need your help with the Debate Club posters," Pam had pleaded. "Don't go running off again!"

"Sorry, I have to get a lot of stuff done before my boss arrives," I said.

"But you kept running out on me all last week," Pam complained. "All the members of the Debate Club are supposed to be helping, you know. We want to make sure the debate with St Ignatius is well publicized!"

"I said I was sorry," I repeated, "but work does have to come first, you know."

"This job seems to have taken over your life," Pam said, eyeing me seriously. "Don't you think you've maybe taken on a little too much? You can't afford to let your schoolwork slide so much."

"I won't," I said. "But I have to work extra hard these first weeks to get the hang of the job."

Pam giggled. "How hard can it be to learn to put plates on tables? Come on, Debbie. The Debate Club really needs you."

"I might have to drop the Debate Club," I said. "I don't see how I can fit it in with work."

"Drop the Debate Club?" Pam exclaimed. "But, Debbie, you love debating."

"It was fun," I said uneasily. I had a feeling I could be talked into choosing the Debate Club over practising hamburger tossing, "but a job is more important to me right now. Debating is . . . well, it's only a school club after all. It won't matter one bit ten years from now whether we debated or not!"

As I drove down the canyon to the café, I couldn't believe I'd said that! I was beginning to sound like Joe! Maybe I'd said it more to convince myself than to make an excuse to Pam, because I did mind, terribly, missing helping with the posters. Debating was one of the things I was good at. I loved that battle of wits, coming up with the clinching argument, feeling good about winning. Maybe I'd be able to make time for clubs and things again, when things settled down at the café. But for now, I was willing to sacrifice anything – absolutely anything – to make sure that Joe did not win his crummy bet!

The café was deserted. I let myself in through the front door and stood there, taking in the squares of sunlight falling on the tables, the friendly silence, the lingering smell of food and coffee. I could easily see how this place could become a haven – somewhere people came to get away from life and its problems. I had been around long enough to notice that most customers came in more to sit and talk than they did to eat. About five or six o'clock, there were lots of hamburger orders, but by eight most kids only wanted a soda or an ice cream or hot chocolate and, on the strength of that order, they sat around talking, sometimes until closing time. I had never stayed that late yet. Joe had always let me go home. Although I thought that many of their conversations were dumb, that they laughed at really stupid things, I sometimes found myself wishing that I could be part of one of those noisy, laughing tables of kids, instead of being the outsider who just served the food. I didn't want to be like them, but the idea of belonging, of having a place where you were known and liked, was very appealing. Right now I didn't feel like I belonged anywhere any more.

I let myself lapse into a daydream in which I stepped into the café and a noisy group immediately called me over. "Hey, Deb, we've been waiting for you. What took you so long? We can't wait to tell you …"

I shook myself free of the daydream and reminded myself why I had come down early. I had to get my practising done before Joe arrived. I changed hurriedly into my uniform and went through to the kitchen. There had to be a method of cooking a lot of stuff at once. It was probably just a question of knowing which order to do things in – just a question of practice. I didn't dare really heat up the grill and waste good food but that didn't stop me from going through the motions. I got out some patties and buns and stood the various condiments where they should be.

"Okay," I said to myself. "Two regular burgers, one extra large, all with fries, ready go!"

I slapped the burgers down on the grill, making sure I held them down with the spatula. Once I was sure they were sticking, I put out three plates and put in three imaginary orders of fries.

"Just a question of organization," I said to myself. "The secret of cooking burgers is merely good organization!" I launched into an imitation of those French chef TV shows. "Let us see if ze burgers are cooked to ze perfection! Ah, magnifique! Now I will flip ze burgers – so … all it takes is ze flip of ze wrist – so, … ah, what skill, what fantastique burgers I am creating! Now for ze buns, placed beside ze burgers – so … and ze pickles on ze plates and ze mayonnaise at ze ready … Chef Deborah is about to create another masterpiece of culinary delight! What elegance! Burger a la Debbie! Are ze buns lightly brown? Mais oui – ze are, and ze burgers are juicy and brown? Mais oui—"

I broke off as I heard a noise right behind me. I spun round and saw Joe standing there, stifling a laugh.

"What are you doing?" he asked, trying to keep a straight face.

"Just practising," I said, feeling my face become hot enough to sizzle those burgers.

He walked over to the grill, put his hand on it, and turned back with a huge smile on his face. "They cook faster if you turn the heat on," he said.

I glared at him, trying not to lose my temper and hurl him into the French fryer.

"Why don't you give up and admit this job isn't for you?" Joe asked.

"I don't see anything hard about this job," I said. "All I need is a little practice. That's what I was doing until you interrupted me."

"I think it will take more than a little practice," he said.

"I suppose you were born knowing how to cook hamburgers?" I asked icily.

"More or less," he said. "I can't remember a time when I didn't have to help out at my dad's deli or my grandpa's restaurant. My folks are great believers in family and in hard work. I've worked hard all my life."

"Well, bully for you," I said, "You think you have exclusive rights on the hard-luck story?"

"Don't tell me *you* were washing dishes when you were three years old?"

"Actually I was driving a steamroller when I was one and a half," I said, laying the sarcasm on like molasses. Of course, it would probably go over his head. "They had to lift me into the saddle and put on an extra diaper so the seat wasn't too hard."

"Very funny," he said. So he did get the sarcasm. "What I am saying," he went on, "is that this job requires someone who is used to working. It requires the common sense that all your fancy education can't teach you. You can have your head filled with stuff like Shakespeare and chemistry and things, but none of that is any use when it comes to real life."

"I'm surprised you've even heard of Shakespeare," I said frostily.

"Yeah, I know him. He wrote Charles Dickens ... or was it the other way round?" he asked.

It was my turn to grin. "Actually, he wrote Ernest Hemingway," I said.

"Oh, yeah, that's right. I remember now," he said. "But he didn't know much about cooking hamburgers, did he?"

"Knowing how to cook hamburgers is not the most important thing in the world," I said.

His eyes held mine. "Yeah, but it's a lot easier than having to bend down and pick them off the floor!" he said, looking pleased with himself, as if he scored the winning point.

I glared at him, making him laugh again.

"One day," I said in my proudest voice, "one day we'll be in a situation where I know what I'm doing and you are the new-comer. Then you'll find out what it's like."

"What sort of situation would that be?" he asked easily. "So far, I haven't met anything I can't handle. Or are you going to take me to ballet class? Come to think of it, I don't think I'd be too shabby at ballet dancing. I was pretty hot stuff at basketball, and it's almost the same moves."

"Did anyone ever mention that you are totally conceited?" I yelled, the desire to hit him becoming stronger every minute.

He thought for a minute, then shook his head. "Nope," he said, and turned and walked out of the kitchen. "These bottles need filling, and the tables don't have any napkins on them yet," he called back to me. "Get moving, girl. You talk too much."

"I hate him," I muttered, stomping out of the kitchen with my arms full of ketchup bottles. "Just wait ... one day ..." I ran through the possible scenes of humiliation in my mind: Joe facing me in a debate at school and me crushing him with my witty brilliance, Joe coming to me for a job when I'm a big business executive and me saying, "I don't think you'd ever learn. You see, cooking hamburgers doesn't prepare you for the executive world." This made me feel a little better, but not much.

In the middle of that evening's shift, I went to the closet to get my brush out of my purse. Joe's jacket was on top of my purse. As I moved it, something fell out on to the floor. It was a copy of *A Tale of Two Cities,* with a bookmark stuck in towards the end of it. I felt myself going hot and cold as I remembered what I'd said to him. *But it's his fault,* I told myself. *I shouldn't feel guilty. He was the one who played the dumb idiot and pretended he didn't know who Shakespeare and Dickens were.*

I went back and forth between confronting him about the book and saying nothing. I didn't have a choice, as it turned out, because he came up behind me.

"Oh, thanks," he said. "You've got my book there." He took it from me.

"You're reading that for school?" I asked cautiously.

"Actually, no," he said. "I just felt like reading it again. 1 always saw myself as Sydney Carton. 'It is a far, far, better thing that I do now than I have ever done ...' " he quoted, putting on a noble accent which made him look somehow different.

"So how come you like to act like a dumb dropout?" I asked.

He put the book back. "Isn't that how you see me?" he asked and walked away. It seemed he could score points against me whatever he did!

Around eight, business dropped off and I went home. I had a ton of homework ahead of me: an English essay for which I still had to skim through a couple of books, some chemistry problems that would probably take me all night, and a page of translation in French. My mother wasn't home, but that wasn't unusual these days. She had started her life as a college student, and now when she wasn't at class, she was at the library, preparing for class. She had left me a note saying there was pasta salad in the fridge, but I wasn't hungry. Actually, I had eaten two hamburgers I had dropped on the floor by mistake. With their slightly burned buns, they had taken away my appetite for the night.

I didn't even look at the pasta salad, but I went right through to the bathroom and ran myself a bath, letting the water come within inches of the top. This had become a nightly ritual for me – my only way of unwinding and getting rid of the French fry smell on my hair and skin. I lay back, pretending it was the hot tub we used to have. Mom kept reminding me that our complex did have a sauna and jacuzzi. I'd tried them once, but a horrible old woman had come into the sauna and taken off all her clothes. After that I'd sworn never to go back.

I lay in the tub, feeling the tension slipping away. My eyes kept drooping shut, and every now and then I forced them open again, reminding myself that I had all that homework still waiting to be done. Finally the water got cold enough to make the tub unpleasant, so I climbed out, wrapping a towel round myself, and walked down the hall to the kitchen to pour myself a glass of juice. Being a super-economy model condo, they had built the kitchen and living room all without walls, just the breakfast bar dividing them. As I opened the fridge, I thought I heard a noise, and I glanced across to the living room. A man was sitting on our sofa. He scrambled to his feet.

"Hi," he said.

"Who are you?" I asked, feeling at a great disadvantage with only a towel wrapped round me. True, he didn't look like a criminal. He was middle-aged and mousy looking, with thinning hair and wire-rimmed glasses. He was also wearing a knitted vest. Then I remembered cases I'd seen on television where neighbours talked about mass murderers. They always said, "he always seemed like such a nice, gentle man." *If he takes a step towards me*, I thought, reaching for the plastic juice container, *I'll throw this juice in his face.* I could see the headline: *GIRL FOILS MANIAC WITH PINEAPPLE JUICE.*

As soon as he opened his mouth to speak, I could tell he was more nervous than I was. "Your mother, er, gave me the key and told me to make myself at home while she went to get milk. I – I didn't know anyone was here. She didn't say ... I, er, expect she'll be back in a minute. She said the mini-mart was only on the corner."

"It's okay," I said. "Sit down. Make yourself at home."

He sat, lowering himself cautiously back on to the sofa. I relaxed my hold on the juice container.

"I'm Norman," he said. "Did your mother mention me?"

"No, she didn't."

Uncomfortable silence.

"We're in the same art history class," he said. "It's been a long time since we both were in school, so we thought we'd study together. I expect you know all about studying, right?" And he laughed, a nervous little hee, hee, hee.

"Uh, yeah," I said. "Excuse me. I'm getting cold."

"Er, yes, of course. Don't let me keep you. I'll be just fine here. Your mother will be back very soon, I'm sure. She said she'd only be a moment."

I backed down the hall and shut my bedroom door very firmly behind me. I wished it had a lock because I still didn't totally trust the man. That laugh had sounded unbalanced for one thing. *MANIAC BREAKS INTO HOUSE PRETENDING TO BE FRIEND OF MOTHER*, the headline would read.

Through our paper-thin walls, I heard the front door slam and my mother's bright voice, "Ah, here we are. Now we can have hot chocolate while we study. Isn't that a terribly studenty thing to do? I am just loving being a student, and I'm so grateful that you've offered to help me study for this quiz."

Mumbled reply.

"I'd have asked my daughter, but she's so busy these days, I never even see her."

More mumbles, presumably telling her I was in my room.

"She's here? Did you two meet already? Oh, I'm so glad."

Old Norman must have a very soft voice, I thought, because a cough from the neighbour got through these walls. He really was a super-wimp!

At that moment there was a tap on my door, and my mother poked her face round it. "I'd no idea you were home, honey," she said. "Poor Norman got a terrible fright.

I just gave him a key and told him to go on in! When you're dressed come on out and meet him properly."

"Thanks, but I have a ton of homework to do," I said.

"He's very sweet," she went on. "He saw me floundering in our art history class, and he's offered to help me study. Norman and I are the only two old fuddy-duddies. He's been taking care of invalid parents for years and now that they're gone, he's decided to go back to school. Isn't that wonderful?"

"Er, great, Mom," I said. "Now please, let me get back to my homework or I'll be up past midnight."

"Of course, sweetie," she said. "I'll be making hot chocolate in a while. Would you like to join us?"

"No, thanks," I said. "I'll be too busy."

After she shut the door, I turned my radio up loud. The woman next door would start hammering on the wall any second, but I didn't care. I needed privacy, to sort out my thoughts. Only one week in school and she'd started bringing home men, I thought. What did she know about men? She didn't have a clue – she'd been married for so long, she'd probably bring home the first mass murderer who offered to help her study for a quiz!

It was hard enough coping with my parents splitting up, but I had pictured them both being by themselves, alone, not latching on to other people right away. Not that Norman looked like a potential candidate for involvement. Surely Mom had better taste than that! My dad was tall and muscular and great looking. He exercised and played lots of golf and tennis.

Come on, I reasoned with myself, *she only wants him for his studying skills.*

And yet, she had brought him home. Again I was back in my *Alice in Wonderland* mode, never knowing when the floor I was standing on would start shrinking or just disappear from under my feet.

Chapter Eight

Then finally, miraculously, things did begin to get a little better. It didn't happen all at once, so that I could put my finger on the moment and say, "That's when I realized I had this job licked". But by the end of my second week at the Heartbreak, I'd worked two whole evenings where I didn't let a single burger slide off the grill and nobody called me back to say that I'd given the wrong person the pickle or forgotten the onion rings. Joe must have noticed it, too, because he actually said, "You know, you're not doing too bad."

"Badly. It's an adverb." I no longer passed over opportunities to score a few points.

"I knew that. I'm just doing my impression of a poor Italian café worker," he replied.

"You are not poor," I answered smoothly, my confidence boosted by his raised opinion of me. "I'll bet that bike you ride cost just as much as my car. And your leather jacket – that probably cost over a hundred dollars."

"More like two," he admitted.

"So why do you act as though you're poor?" I demanded. He grinned sheepishly, as if I had struck a nerve for the first time. "I guess it's the way I was brought up," he said. "My parents are always going on about being poor Italian immigrants and how they have to work twenty-four hours every day just to make ends meet, when the truth is they've got a bundle stashed away.

Everything they make gets put away for the big emergency. They are still driving a '69 Chevy, can you believe it?"

"So you ride the bike and wear the jacket to get back at them?" I asked.

He seemed defensive again. His dark eyes looked away from me. "I ride the bike because I want to," he said. He picked up a tray. "You sliced all these tomatoes?" he asked.

"Sure."

He examined them. "You must be getting better at that, too," he said. "I don't see any fingers in with them."

"I thought this place served finger foods," I quipped back. "And anyway, a few slivers of finger might improve the taste."

Joe shrugged, but I knew I'd won. The regulars, too, seemed to have run out of caviar burger and golf cart jokes and were beginning to treat me like a member of the same species. I was beginning to think they were basically a good bunch – most of the time.

Take Ashley, for example. At first I thought she must have skin as thick as a crocodile's – or else she was super-dumb – because she never seemed to mind being teased or being constantly put down by Joe. Then, late on the Friday evening of my second week, I was alone in the café, since Mr Garbarini wasn't feeling well and Joe had wanted to leave early for a date. It was the first time they had dared to leave me alone, and I felt as excited as if I'd won some big prize. They actually trusted me to count the money and lock up. That was something! I was determined to do everything perfectly so that Joe and his grandfather would come in next day and be surprised by how well I'd done. When the last customers left, I cleaned off the counters, made sure the grill and French fryer were unplugged, counted and bagged the money, and went round to do a last check, making sure no lights were left on in the bathrooms. As I opened the ladies' room door, there was a scurrying sound. Whatever it was, it was definitely bigger than a mouse. I leaped backwards, my heart pounding crazily. I realized fully for the first time that I was alone in a deserted café at eleven o'clock at night, that the bathroom window had probably been open all night, and that anybody could have climbed in, planning to wait until I left to burglarize the place. I was torn between confronting the intruder – *GIRL SUBDUES DANGEROUS BURGLAR WITH PLUNGER, SAVES CAFÉ AND WINS ETERNAL GRATITUDE FROM MANAGER JOE GARBARINI.* "We'd have lost everything if it hadn't been for her bravery," Garbarini stated – or quietly going home and pretending I hadn't heard anything. I might well have done the latter, but just then I heard something that sounded like a muffled sob.

"Who's there?" I demanded, switching on the light.

"Only me," said Ashley as she emerged from a stall.

I only barely recognized her. Her heavy mascara and eye makeup had run down her face so that her eyes and cheeks were big black blobs and streaks. She looked kind of like a very sad clown.

"Ashley? What are you doing still here?" I asked. "What's the matter?"

"Nothing," she said, eyeing me warily and trying to slip past me.

"Look, something must be the matter," I said, noticing the hopeless look on her face. "Is there something I can do to help?"

"It's okay," she said in a choked voice. "I just felt too upset to leave, that's all."

"What happened?" I asked, trying to remember if I had heard any particularly bad teasing or any sort of fight that evening.

"You wouldn't understand," she said. "You'd just think I was being dumb."

I hoped my guilty blush didn't show in the dim light. I wondered how often she had caught me rolling my eyes at the silly things she said. "If … if you'd like to talk about it," I said hesitantly, "I promise I won't think you're dumb."

She went ahead of me, out into the brightly lit café, and sank down at the nearest table.

"I don't think I can take it any more," she said, her voice quivering.

"Take what?" I asked gently.

"Joe," she said. "You know where he went tonight, don't you?" she said.

I had a pretty good idea, but I didn't think it would be tactful to say so. "He said he was going out somewhere," I answered. "I didn't really listen."

Ashley looked up at me with big, hopeless eyes. "He went out with Wendy Hofmeister," she said.

"Oh," I answered. I couldn't think of anything else to say. "I don't think I know her."

"Wendy Hofmeister," Ashley repeated. "She just broke up with Todd Williams. I bet she broke up with Todd just so she could go out with Joe."

I still couldn't think of anything to say, so I asked, "Would you like me to make you a cup of hot chocolate? It'll only take a minute to heat up the water."

"Okay," she said. I busied myself with a kettle.

"You know Joe," I said lightly. "He doesn't keep any girlfriend for more than two minutes."

"Usually," she said. "And each time he breaks up with someone, I think I might stand a chance next. But now – Wendy Hofmeister. Those two have always had a special thing for each other. Everyone knows it. She only went with Todd Williams to make Joe jealous. Todd's Harbor High's star running back … oh, it's totally hopeless. They'll never break up. I'll never get him now."

I came over and sat down opposite her. "I know how you must be feeling, Ashley," I said. "It's really hard to love someone when they don't love you. But you'll meet someone special one day, I know you will. Someone who thinks you're special, too. Joe's really conceited, you know. You deserve someone better."

"He's not really conceited," she said. "He just acts that way. He needs someone who loves him and I'm the perfect person. I'd make him feel special, I'd worship him! But he hardly even notices I exist . . . and when he does—" she started to sob again—"and when he does, it's just to get a laugh out of me."

"So why waste your time on someone who puts you down?" I asked. "Find yourself someone who worships you, too."

"I can't help myself," Ashley said. "I keep telling myself it's hopeless, but I can't stop thinking about him. And besides, my horoscope said that this was my week for a big romance."

I poured hot water into a cup and stirred Ashley's cocoa. "Here, drink this," I said, "and then I'll walk you to your car."

"I don't have a car," Ashley said.

"How are you going to get home?"

"I usually get a ride with Howard or one of the guys," she answered, "but I guess it's too late for that tonight. I can hitch up to the main road."

"You can't hitchhike at eleven o'clock at night," I exclaimed in horror. "Where do you live? I'll drive you home."

She looked up at me through her hair. "I don't really want to go home," she said.

"But your parents will be worried about you, won't they?" I asked.

"It's just my mother, and she'll probably have Jose there again," Ashley said and the same hopeless look returned to her eyes. "They don't want me there. Sometimes he gives me twenty bucks to stay out."

"Where do you go?" I asked, amazed.

"Sometimes I go to a girlfriend's house. Sometimes I just hang around. The video parlour stays open all night." "That's awful, Ashley."

"It's not so bad." She shrugged her shoulders. "He doesn't hit me or anything."

"So where do you want to go tonight?" I asked. "I really should be getting home or my mom will be worried."

"You can just leave me here," she said.

"I can't do that. I promised to lock up. I couldn't leave you inside."

"Okay. Then I guess I'll go home," she said. "They'll be in bed by now anyway. I can just sneak in."

So I drove her home. She lived on a block of old Spanish-style buildings just off Main Street.

"You're nice," she said as I parked in front of her house. "I thought you were going to be real snobby when I first saw you, but I think you're a very nice person. I hope you stay and Joe doesn't manage to get rid of you."

"Oh, he's not going to win his bet, that's for sure."

As I drove home my head was a jumble of thoughts about Joe and his stupid bet and his new girlfriend and poor old Ashley, who had nowhere to go and nobody to lean on. My problems didn't seem as gigantic as they had seemed before. At least my parents hadn't ever paid me twenty bucks to get lost.

I found out the next day that Jose was actually Ashley's step-father. He and her mother had been married for two years, but Ashley hadn't managed to accept the fact that he was there to stay. I'm not sure how much of the not being wanted was real and how much was in Ashley's imagination, but nobody seemed to care if she'd hitchhiked up the canyon so maybe she was right after all. I guess that evening with Ashley opened my eyes, maybe even helped me to grow up a little. Until then I had thought the crowd at the Heartbreak did nothing but laugh and clown around – and tease me, of course. But now I began to look at them differently. Some of them chose to stick around a café because they weren't wanted anywhere else. They weren't as tough as I'd thought they were.

The opening up worked both ways. Ashley no longer looked at me suspiciously all the time, and she even fed me the latest gossip about Joe and Wendy. I don't know why she did this – it clearly hurt her to talk about them – but it sure gave me some good material for my fights with Joe.

Actually, going with Wendy had made Joe pretty mellow. Wendy was a cheerleader and a Very Popular Person at their school, so he was strutting around like a peacock, basking in the glory of going out with her. This meant, of course, that he acted even more conceited than normal.

On Saturday I agreed to work late for him and caught him coming out of the men's room actually wearing a white shirt. I couldn't resist the opportunity.

"Whoa!" I called after him. "Finally I've discovered the truth about Joe Garbarini. He's a closet executive! Are you sneaking out to the future lawyers' club by any chance?"

For once he looked really embarrassed. "Knock if off," he said.

I went on grinning. "Don't tell me you're trying to upgrade your image. Trying to make me feel more at home here?"

He glared. "If you must know," he said, "I'm going out to dinner with Wendy's folks, and I want to make a good impression.

My grin broadened. "Local girl tames wild biker," I said.

"Will you knock it off?" he said. "Just because I happen to be dating the sort of girl who likes me to look good. Your Mr Perfection isn't the only one who can wear clean shirts, you know." He started to take his stuff out of the locker. I could almost hear the cogs turning in his brain to come up with a winning point against me. "Actually," he said, turning back to me with a grin of his own. "I'm beginning to believe this Mr Perfection doesn't exist. How come we never see him?"

"I've never seen Wendy either," I said. "Maybe you're just making her up."

"Oh, no, she's very real, believe me," he said with a very satisfied smile.

"Well, Grant's very real, too," I said. "It's just that ... this isn't his kind of place."

"So what does he think of your working here?" Joe asked. "What does he think of your working, period? I bet none of the other girls he knows work."

"Grant doesn't try to rule my life," I said, not wanting to admit that for the past two weeks I had stalled about telling him I had a job. "We let each other have enough space."

"How come you're working late on a Saturday night?" Joe asked. "That sounds like a little too much space to me."

"The tennis team had an away game," I answered, feeling slightly uncomfortable and wishing I had just let Joe sneak out in his clean shirt after all. "They don't get back until late. We're going to spend tomorrow together."

"Oh, the tennis team," Joe said, with a phony upper-class accent. "How very charming."

"Look," I said angrily. "I don't make fun of Wendy the cheerleader – 'Give me a H, give me an A ...'"

This did not phase Joe one bit. "She does it much better," he said. He picked up his helmet. "Gotta go," he said. "Can I trust you not to burn the place down?"

"You'll have to if you want to meet Wendy," I said sweetly. He gave me a final glance and went out. Our verbal tennis matches were becoming less one sided. He always managed to annoy me, but at least I didn't let him win in straight sets any more.

The thought of tennis matches brought my mind back to Grant. For the past two weeks he had been very busy.

Apart from that one night at the movies, we had only seen each other for a quick snack at the deli and only talked on the phone a couple of times. As great as he was, Grant loved to talk about himself, so it wasn't hard to steer the conversation round to how the tennis team had been doing or how the plans for the senior ball were coming along. And I found enough to say about my days at school to keep him from getting suspicious. But, of course, he'd have to know about my job pretty soon. I worried that one day someone we knew would come into the café or see me getting into my car there and the truth would come out. Then Grant would be hurt and mad that I hadn't told him.

The trouble was, even after a year of going out together, I wasn't sure how he'd react. Grant always presented the image of being confident, even-tempered, wise, and mature, and even to me he never let this image slide. I'd never seen him look less than perfect or lose his temper over a little thing. Even when he'd just lost a tennis game, he was fair and calm to the point of being annoying – especially to a person like me who got worked up pretty easily. But every time I was about to lose my cool with him, I'd remind myself that an ordinary junior does not get a boyfriend like Grant Buckley every day. I'd lost most other things I'd cared about in the past couple of months – one thing I was not going to give up was Grant!

All evening I went through the possibilities, thinking up unique ways to tell him: Well, we have this neat project in sociology class – we're studying how various social groups interact in a neutral setting. That sounded convincing, didn't it? I wasn't even taking sociology. Could I make it biology? We're doing an experiment to see if people are more social than rats? Or maybe I could claim that our church youth group was doing a charity project, learning to be of service. Or even that my dad was thinking of investing in this restaurant and wanted to see first-hand if it was cost effective. The ideas were fun while I toyed with them, but when I seriously considered telling these stories, they all left a bad taste in my mouth. After all, why should I be ashamed to tell someone that I was working because I needed to? It was an honest job, there was nothing shameful about it. "Grant," I'd say, "I'm helping out some friends at a little restaurant. It's great fun and I get to play with the French fryer." He'd probably be too busy to come down and see me there anyway, and by the time school was over I'd have moved on to a better job. Wouldn't I?

I resolved to tell him next morning. He came to pick me up around ten, dressed in his tennis gear, looking like a poster for Young WASPS of America – clean cut, healthy, strong ... I'd never really noticed how he looked before, but now I could almost see Joe's sideways grin as Grant vaulted the low wall and ran easily up our front path.

"You and I haven't played tennis in a while," he said. "I thought you might like to play today. It's a gorgeous morning."

"I'm so rusty," I said. "You'll cream me. I haven't played in weeks."

He smiled affectionately. "I'll be gentle on you," he said, "and it's important not to let your tennis go. You're so good. I thought you might not be getting in enough practice down here."

"I'd feel funny going to the club," I said slowly. "Now that I'm not a member any more."

"You're my guest," he said firmly, as if the club would definitely roll out the red carpet if I came with him. "I've already signed for a court at eleven." He perched himself easily on one of our kitchen stools. "Go get your tennis things. I thought afterwards we could have a snack at the clubhouse and then maybe just lounge round the pool – unless you'd rather go back to the pool at my place. I just want to get some sun. I thought I was looking at a ghost-fish in the mirror this morning."

Since he was a gorgeous golden colour all over and I, who had had no time for sun all spring, was still the colour of dough, I didn't say anything. It was clear that Grant wanted to play tennis and lie in the sun, and Grant usually did what he wanted to. Besides, it might be a good time to slip out my news while he was half-asleep at poolside.

I experienced second and third thoughts as we drove through the brick gateway to the country club. *What am I doing here?* I asked myself. *I don't belong here any more. I'm just going to feel out of place and embarrassed.*

In the locker room I met some girls I knew. They seemed surprised and pleased to see me, but I wondered what they'd whisper to each other as soon as I left. I no longer felt at ease in the place where I had spent a good part of my life until now. I heard double meanings in the most innocent remarks and crept through the foyer like an intruder. Out on the courts I was horribly conscious of my pale legs and arms next to all those tans. Everyone was very nice to me, which made it even worse, somehow, as if I were the token poor person they'd let in and they were proud of their good deed. This might have been all in my head, of course, but all the changes in my life were new enough for me to be sensitive.

Grant and I started to volley. It felt good to hit the ball across the net with a satisfying thwack. I wasn't nearly as rusty as I had thought.

"Hey, not bad!" Grant called when I made him run.

I began to feel more hopeful. I'd make the tennis team again next year, maybe even get a scholarship on my tennis playing. I'd work out at the crummy condo courts. Perhaps there were even some good players down there.

"It feels good to be out here hitting," Grant shouted to me. "Takes away the tension, doesn't it?"

I nodded. I was feeling less tense by the minute.

"Big fight in our house this morning," Grant went on. He seemed to have the energy to carry on a normal conversation while still whacking a ball back and forth. "My sister Kim is home from college for the weekend, and she announced that she's going to be away for the summer – working as a waitress in Yosemite National Park." Thwack. "Good shot."

He stooped to pick up the ball.

"So? What was the fight about?" I asked, standing ready for his serve.

"My dad's furious," Grant said. Thwack. I returned it. "He'd planned for her to spend her summer in a congressman's office in D.C. She said she wanted fresh air and nature, and he said a fat lot of nature she'd get slaving away as a waitress!"

Grant came up to net and put away the ball into a corner. "Good shot," I called. "So what happened?"

"He said he didn't mind the nature bit, but couldn't she be a counsellor or ranger or something? He wanted to call a friend at the Department of the Interior. He said he hadn't raised children to be waitresses! He was very angry. Lots of shouting."

"But it's only a summer job," I said unsteadily. "What's the big deal? She's earning money and doing what she wants to do."

Grant looked at me in surprise. "My parents can hardly tell their friends they've paid for their daughter to go to Sarah Lawrence and the only job she can find is as a waitress, can they? I mean, you can't find a much less prestigious job than waiting on people, washing tables ..."

I saw the look on his face. To him being a waitress was obviously only one step above being a beggar. I swallowed hard, my face suddenly flushing bright red. I swung at a ball and missed.

"You're not concentrating," he called. "That was an easy one."

I walked to the back of the court and picked up the ball I had missed. I would just have to bluff what I was doing with all my time. I could invent visits to the library, term papers, errands for my mother – because there was no way I could tell Grant about the Heartbreak now!

Chapter Nine

It was really strange for me, going straight from school to the Heartbreak. The school I went to could be very snobby and all the kids from the country club went there. It was the sort of school where you had to dress a certain way and drive a certain sort of car to be accepted. At the Heartbreak, it was different. The only people they didn't like down there were phonies. You could be a genuine weirdo and everyone would like you, but they didn't like the sort of people who rode around with Save the Whales bumper stickers and still treated other humans like dirt. When I got in my car and drove out of the school gates, it was as if I were switching personalities and I found it hard to remember which Debbie was which. The problem was that I wasn't sure which Debbie I wanted to be. I didn't belong to either world. I was a former member of one and maybe a future member of the other – maybe. I could see a phoniness in my school crowd I hadn't seen before, and yet I couldn't exactly see myself becoming like Ashley, either! This made life very confusing.

Occasionally the two worlds overlapped, which made my life more confusing than ever. One evening I was waiting tables and Joe was cooking, which was how it mostly was these days because we both admitted he made better burgers than me, when a noisy group came in. They were making loud jokes about what a dump the café was and how brave they were to be here as they settled themselves in the corner booth. When I went to get their order, I recognized them. They were from my school. One of the girls I even knew slightly. Her name was Minda, and she was a cheerleader. I had always secretly admired her because she always looked so perfect. She could be out on the football field or walking round the halls at school and she'd never have a hair out of place, her makeup would be perfect, and her clothes would look as if they'd come straight from the cleaners. My own hair was light and flyaway, and had to be kept in place with large barrettes or bows. It always made me green with envy that someone else could jump up and down in a howling gale at a football game and still look perfect. Because Grant played football, I'd been at parties with Minda, too, but we weren't exactly big buddies. I wasn't quite sure how to handle this now and decided not to say anything.

"Are you ready to order?" I asked.

"Er, sure, what are you having, Minda?" one of the boys said. They didn't even look up at me. I was a nonperson to them.

"I'd like a natural soda," Minda said. "Passionfruit and lime, I think."

"I'm sorry, we just carry regular sodas," I said politely. She looked at one of the boys and laughed.

"They just carry regular sodas," she said, as if I'd said something very funny.

"Well, I told you," the boy said with a grin. "Okay, bring us two regular sodas – lemon-lime. What about you, Todd?"

"A double cheeseburger and hot chocolate."

"I'll have a plate of fries and some iced tea," the other girl said.

"Oh, iced tea, that sounds good," Minda interrupted.

"So you'd like that instead of one of the sodas?" I asked, trying to write all this down.

"Yeah, maybe. Let's see ... and a salad? Can you make me a salad?"

I quickly decided that I could probably toss together some lettuce and tomatoes. "A green salad, sure."

"No pasta?"

"No pasta."

She sighed loudly. "Okay, make it a green salad."

"Oh, I'll have a green salad, too," the other girl said.

"As well as the fries?"

"No, instead of."

"And I want a Chocolate Madness," the last boy said. "Oh, a Chocolate Madness – that sounds wonderful," Minda bubbled.

"Okay, let me get this straight," I said, trying my best to keep track of things. "You'd like two herb teas, one soda, one hot chocolate—"

"Make that two hot chocolates," the boy said.

"And two green salads and two Chocolate Madnesses?" I asked.

"Only one," Minda said. "I didn't say I wanted one."

"I'm sorry, I thought—" I began, when she drummed her fingers on the table.

"Is it really worth waiting round here when it's going to take them hours just to get our order right?" she said with another exaggerated sigh. "Anyone would think we were ordering a three-course meal instead of a couple of snacks!"

"I'm hungry. I don't want to go somewhere else," the first boy said.

"If you wouldn't keep changing your mind every two seconds," I began, "it wouldn't take so long. I'm trying to write down what you want."

"There's nothing difficult about it," Minda snapped. "Any idiot can take a simple order. Just make an effort to listen this time!"

Joe appeared at my shoulder.

"Problem?" he demanded.

I was trying to keep my temper and the thought of Joe yelling at me was almost the last straw.

"You see they—" I began, but Minda cut in.

"We're just trying to order a few snacks but the waitress can't seem to get our order straight!"

"There's no need to yell at her," Joe said with authority. "She hasn't been working here long. It's not easy to keep straight what people want when they haven't made up their minds before they order. Now, if you'd like to take a couple of seconds to figure out what you want, I'll come back and take your orders myself."

He put his hand on my shoulder and steered me away. "T-thanks," I stammered, still in shock that he had actually stuck up for me.

He shot me a triumphant grin. "That's okay. We can't all have brains big enough to take in five orders at once," he said. "Strange, though. I thought you spoke their language – snobese?"

"I know one of them," I said, letting him get away with the putdown for once. "The one who was yelling at me. She didn't even recognize me."

"Spoiled brat," he muttered, glancing back at Minda. "They think they're so cool for slumming it. They'll probably be bragging at school tomorrow how they tried quaint old hamburgers instead of sushi!"

I didn't say a thing. He was probably right. They would be laughing about this place at school tomorrow, and about how the dumb waitress couldn't even remember their order ... and it would never once enter their heads that the dumb waitress was a person, too – a person they actually knew.

At school the next day I passed Minda in the hall and she didn't even bat an eyelid. She just murmured hi to me and my friends. I began to feel guilty, wondering how many times I'd been in a place and lost my temper with the person behind the counter because I thought they'd been slow. I had never thought of them as real people either.

Because of Minda's reaction to the Heartbreak, I wasn't at all sure that I wanted Pam to come see it. She had been getting more and more interested in what went on and kept dropping hints about coming there to see for herself and sample the Chocolate Madness. Pam wasn't anything like Minda, but she was kind of an intellectual, used to travelling round the world and seeing foreign films. I didn't want her to think the Heartbreak was funny – or sad.

In the end I couldn't keep her away any longer and she showed up on Wednesday evening. Wednesdays were usually quiet – unless it had been an especially good day for surfing – and tonight only a few regulars were there. I introduced Pam to them and then had to go right to work in the kitchen, where the French fryer was again giving us trouble. It had been acting up recently, and Joe was continually bugging his grandfather to get a newer model. Joe worked the fryer and I did the rest of the stuff. When I brought out the orders, Pam was sitting with the others, laughing and talking as if she had known them her whole life.

"Did you know," Ashley was saying, "that if you break chocolate chip cookies first and leave them a while, the calories escape and then you can eat them?"

I expected Pam to splutter into her drink or lecture Ashley about what calories really were, but instead she looked really interested. "Is that a fact?" she said, looking up at me with a huge grin. "I've been waiting all my life for somebody to tell me that." I put a large Chocolate Madness down in front of her. "Does it work for Chocolate Madness, too?" she asked.

"You girls and your diets," Howard said, leaning towards Pam the way he always did when he spoke to someone. "I saw the perfect diet on a movie last night. It was on the late, late show and these creatures come out of the drains and eat people's toes and fingers."

"Euww, Howard, you are being disgusting again!" Ashley said.

"They ate a lot but they didn't get fat at all," Howard said happily. "They were skinny enough to go back down the drains. Maybe you should try it, Ashley."

"I think I saw that movie," Pam said. "Don't you remember, Deb – on the late show when you were sleeping over once. You hid in your sleeping bag."

"I remember hiding in my sleeping bag during several late shows," I said. "I haven't got your strong stomach."

Pam turned back to Howard. "Wasn't that the one with the fat chief of police, and the monster gets him while he's taking a shower? That was so funny."

"Yeah, wasn't it great?" Howard asked, his eyes shining. "That is one of my all-time favourites. It's just the right combination of funny and scary."

"That's how I like them, too," Pam answered.

I stood there watching Pam with astonishment. She was always kind of shy around school. Here she seemed to fit right in, laughing and talking as if she were with old buddies. As the evening went on, Art put his arm round her and I even watched Joe tell her that, being Italian, he liked his women with lots of curves. I was sure Pam, a proclaimed feminist, would take that as a sexist remark, but she blushed and giggled, so I guess she liked it.

Next morning at school she grabbed me. "Last night was just great, Debbie," she said. "What a neat place."

"I guess you had a good time," I said with a grin. "What did you think of the gang?"

"They were interesting," she said. "You could write a book about that place. And you know the strangest thing? I didn't feel out of place there. I think you're lucky to work somewhere where you can be yourself and nobody cares. Those people – it didn't matter to them that I dress like this instead of being trendy. When the guy came in from the auto shop – Terry, right? – nobody cared that he had grease all over him."

"I could see you playing along with Ashley about her diets and with Howard about his horror movies," I said.

She grinned. "I wasn't playing along," she said. "I love that idea about breaking chocolate chips before you eat them and letting the calories escape. I've been waiting all my life for someone to tell me that!" She burst into happy laughter. "And the horror movies," she went on. "I've never been in a group where I could admit I liked horror movies before. If you say you like something like that round here, people think you are weird. I'm classed as a brain at this school so I have to act like a brain. That's why I think the café is so neat: nobody put me into a category and made me stay there. I can't wait to go back!"

I wrestled with my mixed feelings. I knew Pam didn't make friends that easily round school, so I was glad for her that she'd enjoyed herself so much. But I wasn't at all sure that I wanted her hanging out at *my* café. I was even surprised at myself that I thought of it as my café. After all, they might have been nice to Pam, but Joe still had labelled me a snob. I didn't want Pam to go and have fun there. If the regulars wouldn't accept me, I didn't want them to accept Pam either.

But Pam obviously didn't notice from my face that anything was wrong because she went on talking excitedly as we walked to our lockers. "And Joe!" she said, beaming at me. "Isn't he something? That guy is definitely cool! What a hunk! Does he have a girlfriend, by any chance?"

I looked at her in complete surprise. "*You* are interested in *Joe*?" I asked, shocked.

She blushed. "You have to admit he's pretty sexy," she said.

"I can't believe what I'm hearing!" I stammered. "Pam, that guy is Mr Macho in person. He thinks God created man and then he rested. Women just evolved from slime much, much later."

"I'm sorry. I know he gives you a hard time and that sometimes he can act like a caveman." Pam grinned. "But I don't care. He's still sexy," she said.

"This is coming from someone who is planning on going to Georgetown University and forging the political future for our nation!" I said, shaking my head in disbelief.

Pam giggled. "I can't help it. He makes me feel feminine and I like it," she said. "He's not at all how you described him. I was expecting someone totally obnoxious. I think you were just trying to keep him for yourself."

"No way," I said firmly. "Anyway, he has a girlfriend. Her name is Wendy and she has lots of frizzed-out blonde hair and huge blue eyes and about three hundred perfect teeth."

Pam gave me a sideways looks. "Sounds to me like you're jealous," she said.

"I think Grant is far more gorgeous," I said. "Why would I need to look at anyone else?"

"So you wouldn't mind if I went after Joe?" she asked.

"Sure I would, but only because you're my best friend and I wouldn't wish him on my worst enemy," I answered. "If you're prepared to be walked all over, go ahead. But I'm warning you, you'll have to fight Ashley for him —and half the girls who come to the café."

I thought Joe would have forgotten all about Pam, but he mentioned her to me when I saw him Friday night. "Where's your friend tonight?" he asked, looking round – somewhat hopefully, I thought.

"My friend? You mean Pam?"

He gave me his crushing look. "How many other friends have you brought here?" he asked. "Of course Pam."

"She's studying," I said. "She's a real brain."

He gave me a meaningful look. "She thought I was pretty hot stuff, right?"

"She's smart, but not when it comes to boys," I said smoothly. "She's partially blind, too."

"You mean she's got good taste, don't you? She knows a great-looking, fun guy when she sees one – unlike other people I could mention!"

"Hmmmph!" I said, because I couldn't think of anything crushing enough.

Delighted to see he'd finally left me speechless, he went on. "I must say I was surprised. I'd never expected one of your friends to be like that. I mean, she acted like a normal person. I expected all your friends to be snobs, like those kids who came in here the other day."

"I don't see why," I said, giving him my frosty stare. "I don't act like a snob."

"Oh, no?"

"I don't!"

"Do, too."

"Like when?"

"Okay ... who has to use big words all the time then explain them to me?"

"Only because I can't converse in grunts. And anyway, I'm getting along fine with everyone else here."

"I guess you do actually speak to us now. When you first came here, you looked at all of us as if we had just crawled out of the nearest pond."

"I did not!"

"Did, too!"

I turned away. "Oh, this is becoming too childish," I said. "I can't talk to you like a regular person. You always resort to kindergarten behaviour."

"Meaning what?"

"Meaning you act like a little kid."

His eyes were calculating. "Oh, and who danced up and down and waved her arms, screaming, 'You're parking in my space'?"

"And who wouldn't move?"

"I didn't have to. It was my space," he said.

This intellectual discussion was prevented from continuing when customers started arriving and neither of us wanted to be caught sounding like a five year old in front of other people. So we went to work, chopping noisily and glaring at each other across the kitchen.

"I bet your friend Pam doesn't fight all the time," he said under his breath, as he tossed a hamburger expertly on to the grill. "She seems like a nice, soft, gentle ... feminine girl to me."

I brought the cleaver crashing down on some onions, sending onion juice spurting up and making myself cry.

"That's probably because she gazed at you adoringly," I said under my breath. "She doesn't have a boyfriend, so she's grateful for any attention ..."

Joe slapped another hamburger on to the grill. "I'm dying to meet your boyfriend," he said. "How come he never comes to visit? Ashamed of seeing you slumming it here?"

"He's too busy with all his activities," I said. "He leads a full life – but then he needs to because he's going places next year."

"Working for Greyhound?"

"Try going to Harvard."

Joe laughed to himself, which I found very annoying.

"I can't wait to meet this Mr Perfection," he said, still giggling to himself. "He's probably a lifelike android. He'd need to be to put up with you."

"Strangely enough, I'm usually known as a nice, kind person," I said, "and Grant and I never fight."

"Like I said, he's a robot," Joe muttered, tossing a hamburger expertly.

"You're the only person I ever fight with," I answered, sweeping my pile of onions into a bowl with one giant swoosh. "I guess you must just bring out the worst in me." Our conversation was broken into again because somebody was selfish enough to ring the bell for service, but we kept it up most of the evening, thinking up newer and juicier things to say to each other each time we passed. Just before I was due to go home, we had a big run on hamburgers and fries, and, right on schedule, the French fryer went berserk again – forgetting to switch itself off and filling the kitchen with black smoke and cremated fries.

"It's the thermostat," Joe growled. "Look at this oil – it's ruined. It's full of burned pieces. We'll have to drain it and start over. Get me that bucket."

"Me?" I asked.

"Well, I can't drain it alone."

"But it will still be too hot."

"I can't help it. We won't have time to do it tomorrow. I want to drain it and get the thermostat out tonight, so I can replace it by tomorrow."

I handed him the bucket and he started to scoop out the hot oil.

"Be careful with that stuff," I warned. "It looks pretty lethal to me."

"I know what I'm ... ouch!" he muttered.

"What happened?"

"Nothing."

"You burned yourself, didn't you?"

"No, I didn't."

"Look, you got oil on your hand. Run it under cold water, quickly."

"Don't tell me what to do."

"Okay, let the skin shrivel up and fall off your hand. It's all the same to me."

"I'll put some butter on it," he said, making a face. I could tell the burn really hurt. He opened the fridge. "We've only got margarine. Will that do?"

"Fat is the last thing you should put on it," I said, taking the margarine away from him.

"Hey, give me that!" he shouted. "My mother always puts butter on burns."

"Maybe so, but it's been proven that it doesn't help and actually causes infections. You need to run it under cold water. Every minute you wait will make the burn worse."

He scowled at me, but turned on the cold water. "It stings," he said.

"Of course it stings, don't be such a baby."

"How long have I got to keep it here?" he asked.

"Until it feels numb."

"What will that mean?"

"That your hand's dropped off," I said, giving him a sweet smile.

"Ha, ha. What are we going to do about the maniac fryer?"

"That oil is obviously too hot to drain. We'll just have to leave it until tomorrow."

"But what about that thermostat? We should take that out tonight so I can buy a new one tomorrow."

"Tell me where it is. I'll get it."

"You won't be able to reach it. It's kind of hard to find, and it's in there real solid ..."

"Man's work, right?" I asked with sweet sarcasm.

"You can go ahead and try if you want," he said, looking up from the sink. "I'll keep the water running for you when you burn yourself – although you might want to try the butter."

I reached across to the panel at the back of the fryer. "This little thing here?" I asked, pointing.

"I guess. But you can't reach that far, can you? I don't want to explain to my grandfather that you've been French fried."

"Don't worry," I said, leaning very carefully across the fryer and wrestling with the little panel. I could feel myself touching hot greasy steel. Fat dripped from the hood above me on to my face and hair. I wrenched the panel open and the little unit came out in my hand. I waved it triumphantly. "Here, I got it," I said.

"Hey, way to go!" he said, looking surprised.

I put my hand up and brushed my hair away from my face. "Phew. I feel I've been deep fried," I said.

Joe laughed. "You've got burned oil all over your face now," he said.

"It's okay. I'm going to go home and take a shower," I said. "How's your hand?"

"I think I'll live."

"You will if you don't put butter on it."

"Don't ever tell my mother that," Joe said. He dried off his hand on his apron. "I'll just check and see that everyone's out of here. Could you just do the floor before you go?"

"Okay," I said. He walked out of the kitchen while I cleaned up drips of oil from the floor. I was down on my hands and knees, looking a little like Cinderella, I suppose, when Joe came back in.

"Hey, guess what?" he said, grinning at me like an idiot. "There's a guy out here looking for you and I've got a sneaky suspicion that it's the famous—"

He never finished the sentence. The guy had followed him through to the kitchen. "Grant!" I yelped in horror.

Chapter Ten

Grant looked down at me with a look of utter horror on his face.

"D-debbie?" he stammered. "What on earth are you doing?"

"Oh, hi, Grant," I replied, trying to sound nonchalant. "I'll be with you in a second. I've got to finish this floor first."

"I don't believe it," he muttered, looking at me as if he'd just found me belly dancing. "I stopped by your house because I just found out about this party, and I thought it would be a nice surprise because we haven't been able to spend much time together recently, and . . . your mother said I'd find you here. I thought maybe you'd gone to the beach. I had no idea you'd be, er, scrubbing floors."

"It's a new form of aerobic exercise," I said. I thought I heard Joe snort. Part of me wanted to get out of there in a hurry, but part of me had an absurd desire to giggle. Grant just looked so horrified, so disgusted. I got to my feet.

"Well, I guess it's okay to go, isn't it, Joe?"

"Sure," Joe said. "As long as you've finished scrubbing the floor." He was clearly enjoying this. I could see his eyes flashing the way they did when he thought something was funny.

Grant looked from me to Joe and back again. "Why are you doing this, Debbie?" he asked.

"We're poor now, remember," I said bluntly. "My parents had to live on something, so they sold me as a slave."

I got to my feet, brushing back my greasy hair with my greasy hand. "I guess I'd better go home and change first, huh?"

"Yeah, you'd better," he said with a shudder. "Let's get going. I told Sherry we'd be there round nine."

When we got outside to his Alfa Romeo, he opened the door for me, but stood back, as if he didn't want to brush against me by accident. "You'll excuse me if I don't kiss you right now," he said. "Your face is covered in smudges."

"It's okay," I said, still wanting to giggle. "Do you want me to put newspaper down on the seat first?" I'd said it sarcastically, but he took it seriously.

"Don't worry, the seats are leather. A little oil might even be good for them," he said, slamming the door shut behind me.

He climbed in and we zoomed off up the canyon. As soon as we were clear of the Heartbreak, he turned to me, his eyes filled with compassion. "I couldn't believe my eyes at first," he said, "when I saw you down on your knees in that filthy kitchen . . ."

"It's not normally filthy," I said. "The French fryer broke."

"Debbie," he said, reaching over to take my hand, then having last minute second thoughts and grasping the wheel again, "do your parents know you're doing this?"

Again his voice sounded as if he were asking, "Do your parents know that you are peddling dope?"

"Mom does," I said. "I haven't talked to Dad for a while."

"But your mother," Grant interrupted, "she knows about it and she hasn't tried to stop you?"

I stared ahead into the blackness of the canyon, watching the high beams cut circles of light into the dark night. "She'd hardly want to stop me," I said, "since I'm the only person in the family who's working right now. Besides, I never see her long enough to talk. She's at classes or she's doing homework. The only time she talks to me is to ask me to quiz her on her Italian or to see if we're out of milk."

"You poor thing," Grant said, turning to give me a reassuring smile. "I never thought, not in a million years ... your parents always seemed so reliable. I guess divorce does crazy things to people. But don't worry, I'm here."

I smiled back. "Thanks."

"My family has enough connections. Yours should, too, actually," he said.

"For what?"

"To find you a decent job."

"There's nothing indecent about working at the Heartbreak," I said.

"I didn't mean it like that," he said impatiently. "You know what I meant."

"You meant a job in our sort of environment, working with our sort of people?"

"Exactly," he said, nodding as if I'd said something very wise. "So don't worry about a thing, Debbie," he went on, "because I'll do some scouting round, and I'm sure we can come up with a great job for you, if you really need the money."

"I really need the money," I said, "but there's really nothing wrong with the job I have. I'm just beginning to be some use as a cook and waitress, and the people are fun."

"Maybe it's still a novelty for you," Grant said. "I can relate to that. But after the novelty has worn off, you'll want to be working among normal, pleasant, professional people. Trust me, Debbie."

I knew it would be useless to tell him that I had to prove to myself I could succeed at the Heartbreak, and that, in a weird sort of way, I liked working there. Also that, if I had to work somewhere, I'd really rather work there than in a boutique where all the customers were clones of Minda. I leaned back against the cool leather and let him drone on about what possible jobs I could get that would look good on college applications. We pulled up outside the condo, and I rushed in for a super-quick shower and change of clothes. My mother was nowhere to be seen. She'd left a note saying, "Gone to performance of Antigone at school" stuck to the refrigerator door with a carrot-shaped magnet. She'd already been to an art show and a chamber concert that week. Less than a month in college and she was already in danger of cultural overdose!

Grant complimented me to the speed of my quick change.

"Maybe I should be a stripper instead," I quipped. "I bet I would make more money at that than as a waitress."

"You can't be seriously thinking ... I m-mean, Debbie ..." he stammered, making me realize for the first time that he took most things seriously.

The party was at Sherry Henderson's house, over by the golf course. It was a great big pseudo-Gothic with a couple of turrets and some stained-glass windows, and it looked like something out of one of Howard's horror movies. In fact, with a little fog swirling round outside, it would be just perfect for the place where the couple's car breaks down and they have to spend the night with the mad scientist. There was already a long line of cars in the driveway: Porsches, Corvettes, Mustangs. We had to walk all the way up the driveway and up the steps to the enormous front door. The door was open and music was spilling out, loud enough to make my whole body want to bop to the beat. We stepped inside and were swallowed up into the noise.

In the big family room at the back the dancing was in full swing, complete with a live DJ in the corner.

"You feel like dancing or getting something to drink first?" Grant asked.

"Drink, please. I'm dying of thirst," I said.

He took my hand and led me through to the kitchen, where a keg of beer was balanced on the counter. He helped himself and

I took a can of soda from an ice chest. We had just taken our first sips when Sherry, our hostess, came in, accompanied by a couple of cheerleader friends. One of them was Minda. Minda went right up to Grant and flung her arms round his neck. "Hi, Grant," she said in a squeaky little voice. "I've been looking for you everywhere."

"We just got here," Grant said, looking embarrassed that Minda's arms were twined round his neck. "Debbie had to work late."

"Oh, poor Debbie, where do you work?" Sherry asked. I could feel Minda's eyes on me. Any second she'd recognize me and blurt out to everyone that I worked at the Heartbreak Café. I don't know why it should have mattered that everyone knew, but it did.

"Homework," Grant said, before anyone could say anything. "She had to work late on her homework."

I opened my mouth to say something, glanced across at Grant, then shut it again. Maybe he was wise to have smoothed things over so quickly, and I should have found myself sighing with relief. After all, explaining my job to Minda and Sherry would be an exercise in futility. They'd never understand. It was just that I kept seeing these disturbing pictures of the Heartbreak crowd looking at each other as they sometimes did when a person acted like a phony. I shook my head to clear it.

"Homework's such a drag," Minda said, giving me a commiserating look. "I'll be glad to get out of school in two more months."

"Aren't you going on to college?" Grant asked, sounding surprised.

"Are you kidding? Who wants to waste time in four more years of school?" Minda said. "My parents keep bugging me to go, but I really don't want to. It doesn't make sense, either, because Daddy can get me straight into modelling and that's what I want to do."

"You're lucky you know what you want to do," Sherry said. "I don't. I've put down biology for my college major, but I really don't know what I want to do with it. My father assumes I'll be a doctor like him, but he's crazy. Imagine going to med school for half your life!"

"I'm going to be at law school," Grant said. "That's going to take years of studying."

"Better you than me," Minda said. "Brains like you and Debbie deserve each other. You can both get married and be horribly clever together!"

Grant put an arm round my shoulder. "Not a bad idea, huh, Deb," he said. "You can go to law school, too, and then we can defend difficult cases as a team."

"Not me," I said with a shudder. "There're already too many lawyers in my family."

"What do you mean?" Sherry asked.

"It means her father was a lawyer. He just split with Debbie's mom and left them," Grant said.

"He didn't exactly leave us," I said hurriedly. I didn't want these girls thinking of my father as a flake. "He just found practising law too depressing and soul destroying. I can understand that."

"But what about all that lovely money?" Minda asked. "Doesn't he miss that?"

"Apparently not," I said. "Money never did mean too much to him."

"That would be the only reason I could see for being a lawyer in the first place," Minda said, with a pretty little pout. "Grant, honey, would you pour me a beer?"

"I didn't know you liked beer," Grant said, obediently holding a glass to the keg for her.

"I don't. I simply hate it," she said. "But there's no champagne and we finished the vodka."

"Don't you think you should drink soda or something?" Grant asked.

"Why?" Minda said. "I'm spending the night so I don't have to drive anywhere."

I took Grant's arm. "Let's go dance," I said.

We squeezed into the other room. The noise was overpowering, and I could only dance for a few songs before I thought my head might explode. I dragged Grant outside on to the terrace. A couple was making out on the porch swing, so we tactfully backed inside again. The music was getting even louder, and I began to feel terribly tired.

"Do we have to stay?" I whispered.

Grant looked surprised. "We just got here."

"I know, but I'm tired."

He put on a wise expression. "You work like Cinderella, what can you expect?" he said. "Now you know why she ran home from the ball at midnight."

"Maybe she just found Prince Charming's friends boring," I said.

"Boring?" Grant asked in amazement. "These guys aren't boring, they're fun. You wait and see."

Sure enough, the fun started pretty soon. Denny Ellis did a tightrope walk across the upstairs balcony rail, and a couple of guys had a pillow fight with sofa pillows, which ended when one got thrown in the pool. Soda got spilled on the white living-room carpet. Cigarette stubs got ground into the parquet floor. Glasses got broken. I remembered how many years I'd longed to go to parties like this, parties where the popular crowd from school hung out. It was only since I'd started dating Grant that I had been allowed to attend them. My parents knew Grant's parents and thought he was a good, reliable escort. I'd never really had that much fun at them, either, but I pretended to because everyone else kept saying, "Isn't this fun? Isn't this a blast?" I thought there must just be something wrong with me.

Now I found myself watching as an outside observer. Was any of it really fun? Were these kids really having a good time or were they disguising the fact that they weren't having fun by drinking too much and doing crazy stuff? Nobody here was getting to know anybody else. Nobody was talking and nobody was laughing, except that kind of crazy laughing that accompanied a dumb stunt, like a head-banging contest. I'd taken it for granted that this was my world and these were my sort of kids. Now I found myself wondering whether I wanted to be part of it or not. I'd never had anything to compare it to before. I'd assumed that I must be too immature to appreciate grown-up parties, and that as soon as I learned to like beer, I'd have as much fun as the rest of them. Now, for the first time, I dared admit to myself that I was bored, bored, bored!

I excused myself from Grant and went upstairs to the bathroom. There was a line of people waiting for the bathroom in the hall, so I slipped through to the master bedroom, where I found Minda, Sherry, and a couple of other girls sitting on the floor. Minda was crying.

"What's wrong?" I asked.

Sherry looked up. "She's crying because she used to step on ants in third grade," she said.

"Oh," I answered. I couldn't think of anything else to say.

"You'd cry too if you remembered all those poor little ants," Minda said and broke into loud sobs.

"I think it's just terrible," the girl beside Minda agreed. "Life is so sad."

"All the poor little bald eagles dying out!" the third girl agreed.

I stepped over them to get to the bathroom. When I came out again, they were sobbing on each other's shoulders. It seemed like the right moment to go.

Grant was not at all pleased about driving me home.

"It's really very rude to walk out just when the party is getting going," he said. "People will think we weren't having a good time or something."

"Well, I wasn't," I said. "It was too noisy and too boring."

"I can't see why," he answered. "They're all pretty fun people. You have to make more effort to fit in."

"You mean I have to learn to get drunk?"

He gunned the engine and we shot down the driveway, sending up a shower of gravel behind us.

"Maybe a little beer would have relaxed you," he said.

"Or made me act like a crazy person and walk across the balcony rail?" I answered.

"What is the matter with you?" he asked, turning to me, so that his eyes shone bright blue in the streetlight. "You used to like being with me, I thought. Tonight you hardly even wanted to dance."

"I'm sorry," I said, "but I really wasn't in the mood. That music was giving me a terrible headache."

"Why don't you quit that stupid job right now and we'll try to find you one that doesn't make you so tired all the time?" he suggested.

"I don't want to quit it, and I don't want you to find me a job," I said. It came out much fiercer than I intended.

"I am just trying to help you in a difficult situation, Debbie," Grant said in a hurt voice. "I thought you'd appreciate that."

"And you might appreciate that I want to live my own life," I said. "I'm a big girl now. Apparently I've got to come up with my own money from now on, so it's up to me how I do it."

We drove on in frigid silence.

"Will you be free to come over tomorrow night and watch videos, or will you be too exhausted from your slave labour again?" he asked as he drove into the condo parking area.

He was staring straight ahead, tight-lipped, with a hurt look on his face. I reached over and put my fingers on his cheek. "I'm sorry, Grant," I said. "I guess I have been pretty crummy company lately. It's not easy getting used to all the changes in my life. Of course I'd like to come over tomorrow. I'll get Joe to let me leave early."

He slipped his arm round me. "If only you wouldn't be so pig-headed and let people help you, you'd find life a lot easier," he said. He pulled me towards him so that our faces were only centimeters apart. "I want to help you, you dummy," he whispered, giving me a little kiss on the nose. "I want it to be the way it used to be between us." His lips moved down to meet mine. His arms tightened round me. I tried to relax and lose myself in the kiss the way I used to, but I couldn't. I tried to pretend that there was nothing wrong between us, but I could feel the tension. It was as if someone had put a physical barrier between us. Maybe if we could have come right out and yelled at each other, the way Joe and I did at the café, we could have cleared the air and everything would have been fine. But Grant was not the kind of person who had been brought up to yell. In his world you made polite, icy digs at somebody when you were mad at him. When Grant laughed and said that my neck still tasted of French fries, I used it as an excuse to get out of the car.

In bed I curled into a tight little ball with a bad case of lonely stomach. I hadn't had a good time tonight because I'd been tense and overtired? It couldn't have anything to do with me and Grant, could it? I shut out everything and tried to sleep because I was scared that, if I analyzed it, I might admit that Grant and I were two very different people and that it hadn't just been the party that was boring, but him.

Chapter Eleven

On Saturday morning we got a letter from the family court, saying we'd all have to meet with a counsellor to decide what was best for my future. I thought this was a joke, since obviously what was best for my future would be to have everything back the way it was. I grinned to myself as I wondered what my parents would do if the court ordered them to get married again instantly. The court meeting didn't seem very important to me, but my mother was really mad about it.

"What do they mean by, 'decide your future'?" she stormed. "I hope your father hasn't got some crazy idea about having you come live with him."

Just for a second I pictured living in an artists' colony on the beach, taking long walks, painting, and talking late into the night with brilliant intellectual minds – a life of freedom and self-expression, just as dad wanted it.

"Maybe I should go and live with Dad on the beach," I suggested, "so you can get on with your college studies in peace."

"Don't be silly," she said. "That sort of life would be no place for a young girl."

I turned away and went into my bedroom. She hadn't said she didn't want me to leave, but then I suppose it was becoming more apparent all the time that she wouldn't miss me one bit. We hardly saw each other any more, and when we did we often ended up in a fight. We had been fighting most of the morning until the letter arrived. Like most of our fights, it was over housework. For sixteen whole years my mother had done everything. I would put dirty clothes into my laundry basket and I'd find them hanging up again, freshly ironed, in my closet. I would sit down to dinner every evening to find a complete meal in front of me. Now suddenly my mother expected me to turn into Betty Crocker overnight. She expected me to notice if we were out of anything. One morning earlier that week, I had found my best white blouse crumpled up on top of the dryer. I had nothing else to wear, I was going to be late for school, and I exploded.

"Oh, no, look at this! This is too much!" I yelled.

My mother came running. "What is it?"

"Look at this blouse. I can't wear this!"

"It should have been washed by hand," my mother said, examining it.

"How was I supposed to know?"

"You can read labels as well as anyone else," she said. "It will be okay if it's ironed."

"Can you iron it for me?"

"I don't have time," she said. "I'm due on campus in twenty minutes."

"But, Mom, I'll wreck it," I wailed.

She picked up her purse. "Don't be such a baby, Deborah," she said. "You're sixteen now. It's about time you did some things for yourself."

"It's not my fault you did everything for me until now," I yelled after her as she walked to the door. "I can't turn into an instant expert, you know."

I mumbled to myself all the way through the clumsy attempt at ironing. How could I make her see that she just wasn't being fair? It wasn't that I was unwilling to do my share, I just needed somebody to show me what I was supposed to be doing. And she was never around long enough to do that.

Then on Saturday morning I had woken up to find her already in a cleaning frenzy. "We must get this place in order," she said the moment I poked my head out of my bedroom. "It looks like a slum and Norman's coming over this afternoon."

"Aha. Another cosy little art history assignment?" I asked. I had only said it in fun, intending to tease the way I would have teased one of my friends if they'd had a boy over to work on homework with them, but my mother jumped down my throat.

"And what's so terrible about someone coming over to help me study?" she demanded.

"Hey, calm down, I was only joking," I said. "You can have anyone over you want," I said. "I won't be here snooping on you if your thoughts stray from the history of art."

Even then she didn't smile. "Has it occurred to you that I might be finding college difficult after so many years?" she snapped. "I suppose you think this whole thing is a huge joke – your old mother trying to act like a teenager again?"

"No, I don't think that," I said quickly.

"Then you might be a little more cooperative," she said. "You might help round the house a little more."

"I do have a job," I said. "I'm not home much."

"The job was your choice, remember," she said.

"Sure, my choice if I didn't want to have to walk five miles to school and have nothing to wear and not go to college ... some choice," I snapped.

She pushed back her hair. "Don't try and lay all the guilt on me, Deborah, because I'm dealing with all the worry I can right now," she said.

I opened my mouth to say that she wasn't being fair. That she was expecting me to grow up overnight and that if anyone should be feeling bad right now, it was me, because I was the one who had lost both a father and mother through no fault of my own. But as I watched her race round the living room with a duster, I began to wonder if what she said was true. Was she worrying more than she showed? Was this frantic studying only an attempt to forget that her life had crumbled? Maybe she did miss my father terribly. And I wasn't doing anything to help. As I reached my bedroom I resolved to be nicer to my mom. I didn't know I was being followed until a voice yelled in my ear, "Look at this floor! Every item of clothing you own must be lying on it."

"I like them there," I said. "I know where everything is when I have to get dressed in a hurry."

"But it's a disgrace, Deborah," she said.

"It's my room. Nobody else has to come in here," I argued. "You're not planning to give Norman the grand tour of our stately home, are you?"

We glared at each other.

"You'll be sorry," she said. "One day things will start breeding under all that junk. Don't be surprised if cockroaches start walking over your face one night."

I grinned. "You've said that a million times before," I said, "and it hasn't happened yet."

"That doesn't mean it won't," she said grimly. "Now I want it picked up before you leave this morning. Understand?"

"Yessir! I mean ma'am!" I said, giving her a salute. Even this didn't make her grin, as it definitely would have done in the past. Instead she raised her eyes briefly to the ceiling, as if she thought I was being childish, then hurried back to cleaning the living room. *So much for being nice to my mom,* I thought. *We can't say a thing to each other right now without yelling ... and it's not all my fault. She's the one who's totally grouchy ...*

I flung things into my closet, listening to each item land with a satisfying clunk. I stayed in my room and we hardly said a word to each other for the rest of the morning, until the mail arrived with the summons to court. Then I was glad to escape to the Heartbreak, leaving my mother nervously plumping pillows and waiting for Norman. *At least I don't have to worry about her being alone with that wimp,* I thought. I hoped that Norman wasn't going to become a permanent fixture in Mom's life, because he gave me the creeps. He was always swallowing nervously and you could see his Adam's apple going up and down. He wrung his hands a lot, too. I wondered if he was always nervous or if my mother made him that way. She was certainly making me uptight these days, always waiting to jump on me for the least little thing.

Joe greeted me as I walked in the door at the Heartbreak. "Well, look who's here," he called. "How was your party with the android? He have to go back to Mr Goodwrench for some fine tuning today?"

"Don't you start!" I growled. "I've had just about all I can take today already."

"You and your android have a fight?"

"My mother," I said, flinging my bag into the closet and yanking out my uniform so violently that the wire hangers jangled.

"Oh," he said. "Parents can be a pain, can't they?"

"You can say that again."

"You want to talk about it?" he asked.

"And have you and the others laugh about it all next week?" I demanded, turning to face him.

"Is that what you think I'd do?" he asked, and I thought he blushed a little.

"It's what you've done every moment since I first got here," I said. "You haven't missed one opportunity to make me look bad. I'm sure you could all have a good laugh about Debbie's parents fighting over her in court."

"You have to go to court?" he asked. He was standing right behind me.

"I said I don't want to talk about it, okay?" I muttered, and walked ahead of him into the kitchen.

"Fine with me," he called after me. "I don't go in for soap operas myself."

This exchange had added to the upsets of the morning.

I felt bad about it all afternoon, especially as everyone at the Heartbreak seemed especially nice and friendly for once, joking and kidding around with me as if I were one of them. *Maybe Joe really did want to help*, I thought guiltily. *Maybe I should have told him, and then, he would have understood that I've been having a hard time . . .* Then I pictured Joe listening seriously to everything that's happening in my life, then running out to the rest of the kids yelling. "Hey, guess what she said now, guys: she's part of the property settlement! Her dad gets her Mondays, Wednesdays, and Fridays, unless he's playing golf, and her mom gets her Tuesdays and Thursdays unless she's playing bridge or getting her hair done!" That seemed like just the kind of thing he would do, and I was glad that I hadn't blabbed. *Let them know nothing about me,* I thought. *Let them just learn to like me for myself – the person they see here!* Just like with everybody else at the Heartbreak. I knew nothing important about anybody's life, except Ashley's, and that was my mistake. I didn't even know where anyone else lived or what sort of home life they had. I knew that Joe's mother put butter on burns and that they saved all their money, but nothing else. Not whether he had brothers or sisters or whether he was happy at home.

I realized then that this was part of the appeal of a place like the Heartbreak. When you came here you were a person. If you were a nice person, people liked you. It was a small world, with its own rules, which was why the kids spent so much time there.

The court hearing was set for Tuesday morning. I don't know why I felt so scared about it – only my mother and father and a court-appointed counsellor would be there – but I was as nervous as if I were in there on a murder charge. I suppose I've always been ultra-law-abiding. I even stop at a Don't Walk sign when no cars are coming, and I've never been in trouble with the police. So this was the first time I'd ever been in a courthouse. It wasn't terrible or anything. It was a modern concrete building with a marble floor and lots of wood panelling, but I noticed the armed policemen standing at the entrance and it was all I could do not to run out again.

"This is only a formality," my mother said, although her voice wobbled a little, too. "Just part of the divorce proceedings. We all sit down at a table and decide what's best for you, that's all. We need to get it legally registered in case your father tries any funny business later on."

"What sort of funny business?" I asked, trying to shake an image of my father dressed as a clown from my mind.

She looked embarrassed. "Oh, you know, if he tries to get you to live with him. Tries to turn you against me."

"Dad?" I asked. Were we talking about the same man? A man who was always willing to go along with anything, from going out for ice cream to buying me a new jacket? She made him sound like a monster who was about to kidnap me.

The counsellor was a Mrs Farbstein. She was big and fat and jolly. Too jolly, I thought. Joe would definitely think she was an android. "Court-appointed android," flashed through my mind, and I began to giggle. Everyone looked at me with sympathy.

"This is only a formality, honey," Mrs Farbstein said. "Don't be nervous."

"I hope he shows," my mother said. "I'm missing my Great Operas Workshop."

As if on cue my father came in. It was only a month since I'd last seen him in the flesh but he looked bigger somehow, and more tanned and healthy than he'd been at our last lunch. He was wearing an open-weave Mexican shirt and I could see the hair on his chest because the neck was opened so low. He was also wearing sandals, which he usually only wore on vacation. His eyes lit up when he saw me.

"Hi, Punkin," he said, giving me a big grin. "How's it going?"

"Okay, I guess," I said. "I got a job."

"No kidding, where?"

"I'm a waitress."

"Is that right?" he said, laughing as if I'd said something funny. "Tipped the soup down anyone's neck yet?"

"Tell him where you're a waitress," my mother said sternly.

"At the Playboy Club?" my father asked, showing fake surprise.

"At a café on the beach," I said.

"Sounds okay to me," he said. "I've been hanging out in plenty of cafés on the beach myself. Maybe I should come let you wait on me some time."

"It's really a teen place," I said. "You know, loud music, burgers, that kind of thing."

"I still might come," he said, giving me a conspiratorial wink. "I might meet a cute chick!"

"Peter!" my mother said in a shocked whisper. "We are in court."

My father cleared his throat and walked over to the table. "Oh, yes, I forgot. Court," he said, pulling out a chair and sitting down. "How are you," he said to Mrs Farbstein. "I'm Peter Lesley."

Mrs Farbstein did a lot of talking, lots of legal stuff about rights and duties and welfare. Then she asked me if I was happy with the situation as it was. I looked from my mother to my father. I looked at Mrs Farbstein, who was gazing at me intently, as if she was really interested in what I was about to say. I wondered what they'd all do if I told her I was desperately unhappy and only my parents getting back together again would lift me out of severe depression. I chickened out at the last minute. "I guess so," I mumbled, so quietly that they could hardly hear it.

"You're still getting along fine in school?" she asked.

"I guess so," I said again.

Mrs Farbstein put on her kind-but-efficient face. "I think we all realize that the peer group situation is the most important stability we can offer the teenager," she said. "Changing schools should be avoided above all else, but Debbie's obviously warm relationship with her father should be given ample opportunity to continue. I understand that Mr Lesley has now moved into a suitable apartment and would like legal access to his daughter. I am therefore going to put it on record that Debbie has the court's permission to spend weekends and vacations with her father. Since she is already sixteen years old, the final decision for these visits will rest with her."

Then she got up and began shaking hands all round.

"Waste of a morning," my mother muttered to me. "This was what we'd agreed to anyway." She picked up her book bag. "Now, if you'll excuse me, I've got to rush," she said. "I don't want to miss my next class."

My father caught my eye. "Taking this education seriously, is she?"

"Very seriously," I said.

"But you're getting along all right?" He looked down at me with concern.

"I guess so."

"You've said that twenty times today. Is there anything I can do for you?"

Start acting like my father again! I wanted to yell, but I couldn't. He looked so relaxed, so bursting with health, as if he had blossomed after years of being asleep. Maybe living with us had not been the right thing for him. Maybe all that worry about providing for Mom and me had been destroying him.

"I'd like to come visit you some time," I said.

"I'd like that, too," he said. "Now that I've got a respectable place of my own. It's bigger than a breadbox, but only by about a loaf. You should see the price of real estate down there. It's laughable really. People are renting out garden sheds and other people are crazy enough to want them. But I've got a sofa bed in the living room, so I can put up guests like you. Maybe now that you're working in a café, you can come and cook for me."

"I can do hamburgers," I said.

"Better than me. I'm only up to canned chili," my father said. We grinned at each other.

"I'm sorry to bring you into court like this," my dad said. "It was only a formality really, but I thought I'd better insist on it, just in case your mother tried any funny business."

"What sort of funny business?" I asked warily.

My father looked round, as if he didn't want to be overheard. "Don says that ex-wives can become very bitter and vindictive."

"Don?"

"The guy I shared a place with until I found my own place. He's been divorced for three years and his ex had taken him to the cleaners. She even got the judge to believe that she'd put the downpayment on his sports car. He had to pay her off three thousand dollars just to drive his own car."

"Mom would never be like that," I said.

"I'm sure she wouldn't," Dad answered. "I'm just playing it safe. I just didn't want to find that next year she suddenly decided

I was a bad influence on you and wouldn't let you see me any more."

"I'd still see you," I said. "I'm almost grown up. I can see who I want."

"How about coming down some time next weekend?" he said. "I could do a barbecue and you could make your famous hamburgers."

"How about you make your famous chili?" I said. "I make enough hamburgers all week."

He laughed and put his big arms round me. "I miss you, Punkin," he said.

"You were the one that left," I reminded him.

"My leaving had nothing to do with you," he said. But he said it so forcefully that I couldn't help wondering if I was at least a part of what drove him away.

Chapter Twelve

I had a neat barbecue with my father the next Sunday. His apartment was on a funny old block opposite the beach. It was one of those buildings you only see at seaside towns, like a child's castle made out of pink frosting. It had battlements across the top and a flight of tiled steps leading up through an archway. The steps were open, right up through the building, and as we walked up them our feet echoed.

"Nobody could sneak out of here," I told Dad, and he laughed. He seemed really pleased to see me and had obviously made very sure that his apartment was clean and tidy.

"You can tell Mom I don't live in a pigsty," he said. The apartment was, as he had predicted, not much bigger than a breadbox. Some of our old furniture looked really out of place in the small rooms. There was just one main room, with a kitchen area at one end, and a small bedroom and bathroom off it. You had to go through the bedroom to get to the bathroom, which was inconvenient, but otherwise it wasn't bad. And it had a terrific view. He had a tabletop barbecue out on his little balcony, and we cooked out there, watching the ocean turn pink as the sun set. Dad had brought us two enormous steaks – in celebration of his liberation from healthy food, he said. The old man from the apartment across the hall joined us and brought a big bag of tortilla chips and a very spicy salsa. I offered to make a salad, but Dad said that there was to be nothing healthy in the meal. So we sat together, the three of us, sharing two steaks and hot salsa while we watched the sun set and talked about everything except school and lawyers. The old man, Manuel, was Mexican and made a living creating driftwood sculptures. He showed me some and they were really good – dolphins and seals carved out of the natural contours of the wood. It seemed like a pretty good way to make a living. As I sat there, listening to him and Dad talking, I tried to picture what it would be like living with Dad and watching the ocean at dinner every night. Wouldn't this be just the sort of life I needed right now: no pressure, no schedule, nobody bugging me if I left clothes on my floor? At least he'd notice if I were around. In an apartment that size you couldn't help but notice another person!

"How did your weekend go?" Pam asked when we got together for lunch on Monday. "I called last night, but you must have come back real late."

"It was terrific," I said. "He lives in the neatest little place with a balcony right out over the ocean. We sat there and watched the sun set. I met this old man, Manuel, and after dinner we walked round and saw some of the other people from his building. They're all artists and writers."

"Weird or normal?" Pam asked.

"Very, er, creative," I said. "Some of them are pretty way out. This guy wanted to show me his painting of a nude and he said he hoped I wouldn't be too shocked by it. When he showed it to me, though, it was all squares and triangles with a big splotch down the middle, as if someone had upset the paint, and I couldn't see a person in it at all."

Pam laughed. "What about your dad? How's he doing?"

"He looks relaxed," I said. "As if he's enjoying himself."

"Has he written any screenplays yet?"

"Not that he told me about," I said. "There was a typewriter on the table by the window, but no paper in it."

"I guess it takes time for inspiration to flow," Pam said.

"I guess so."

"Was he glad to see you?" she asked cautiously.

"Very. He treated me like I was a guest and not his daughter. It was funny in a way. He had the place all clean and shining so that I wouldn't tell Mom he lives in a pigsty. I'm thinking of spending the summer with him."

Pam looked surprised. "You are? What would your Mom think?"

I shrugged my shoulders. "The lady at the juvenile court said I could, so there's not much Mom could do about it. Maybe she'd be glad to have a summer without me. She hardly notices I'm there anyway."

"Oh, that's not true, Debbie!" Pam said. She's always had a soft spot for my mother because Mom bakes outrageous blueberry muffins.

"It is so," I defended. "All we do is yell at each other these days. I bet she doesn't even want me around."

Pam laughed nervously. "Come on, Deb," she said. "Think of what she must be going through right now ..."

"What SHE must be going through?" I demanded. "What about me? Whose side are you on, anyway?"

"It's not a question of sides," Pam said. "I know it's really hard for you, but it must be equally hard for her. Even more so. Your dad was the centre of her life."

I made a face. "Well, you don't have to worry, because right now her college is the centre of her life. She's so into this culture stuff that I swear you and I could trade places for a week before she noticed you weren't her daughter."

"I don't believe a word of it," Pam said stoutly.

"It's true," I said, laughing in spite of myself. "I swear it, Pam. You watch next time you come over. Most of her communications to me are notes taped to the refrigerator telling me we're out of bread and she's gone to another concert."

Pam looked as if she only half believed me. There was a pause while she considered the information. Then she asked, "So you really might go to live with your Dad for the whole summer?"

"I might," I said. "Doesn't it sound like a neat idea? Wouldn't it be great to be treated as an adult, to come and go as I pleased, with no schedule and creative people all around me? Who knows, maybe I'd start writing, too."

Pam giggled. "You, writing!"

"Why not?" I answered. "I'm a good writer. We could write a story about high school. I'd put in the teenage stuff, and my dad could add the sex and violence to make it sell!"

Pam laughed. I laughed too, because I hadn't really been serious. But working with my dad on a play did sound like a wonderful idea. We'd both have so much fun and laugh a lot and not take anything too seriously.

"But what about the Heartbreak Café?" Pam asked, popping my daydream bubble. "You've only just started there. You'd have to quit."

"I guess so," I said, mulling over this fact. "But there are plenty of little cafés on the beach where my father lives. I could work in one of them."

"And let the guys at the Heartbreak down?" Pam asked.

"Hey, I don't owe them anything," I said fiercely. "They only pay me four fifty an hour."

"But wouldn't you miss them?" Pam asked. "You talk about them all the time. Wouldn't you miss fighting with Joe?"

"Of course not," I said in horror.

"How is he?" Pam asked suddenly, a soft, dreamy look coming over her face. "Is he still as cute as ever?"

"I don't know why you think he's so cute," I said. "His hair is always a mess, and his eyes are so dark and brooding and he is too ... mean-looking and ..."

"And too gorgeous," Pam finished for me.

"And too conceited," I added.

"Is he still going out with that girl?" she asked.

"Ashley would have told me if he wasn't," I said, "but he doesn't talk about her much."

"I've got to get down there again," Pam said. "If only I didn't have all this homework."

Then the bell rang and we went to our separate classes. But I kept thinking about what we had said all afternoon. It would be fun to spend the summer with my dad, but would I be letting them down at the café? After all, I had sort of promised Mr Garbarini that I wouldn't quit on him, and I hated to let people down. Also, I had to admit, I looked forward to seeing them all, to have everyone look up from the table and hear someone say,

"Here she is. She finally got here!" Of course, Joe was usually ready with some slick remark, but I was learning to ignore his putdowns – when I couldn't come up with a better putdown of my own, that was.

It wasn't that I wanted to be mean to Joe. I wanted to get along with him. It would have been just great if he'd looked up when I came in and said "Hey, who's the great-looking chick?" the way Art did, or "Did you see the rerun of the Twilight Zone last night? It was awesome," the way Howard did, or "Do you know what I just found out about chocolate and acne?" the way Ashley did.

I even joked around myself sometimes, especially when something funny happened. Like that day in P.E. There was a girl in my class called Krystal, and she was everything the Heartbreak crowd expected a yuppie princess to be.

"You're never going to believe this," I announced, when I got to the Heartbreak. Sliding into a seat beside Ashley, I could see the faces round me, eager and interested, waiting to laugh. "The funniest thing happened in P.E. class," I said dramatically. "We were beginning a new segment, and this girl Krystal was furious because she didn't get fencing or archery—"

"Fencing or archery?" Everyone shook their head.

"She wanted something where she could wear a glove because she's just had her nails silk-wrapped," I explained. The laughter began.

"What in the world is silk-wrapped?" Howard wanted to know.

"It's an expensive way of having fake nails put on," Ashley said witheringly. "They're always talking about it in Superteen Magazine."

"I gather it cost her forty-five dollars," I said, "and our P.E. teacher wouldn't switch her out of handball. Of course, the very first game she broke a nail, and boy, was she mad. She threatened to call her lawyer."

More laughter.

"Hey, Lesley!" Joe's voice boomed from the kitchen. "We're not paying you to be the entertainment. I've got a dishwasher waiting to be unloaded. Get in here."

"Oh, come on, Joe," Art said, slipping an arm round my shoulder. "She hasn't finished her story yet, and it's really funny. So what did she do?" He turned back to me.

"Did you ever think," Joe interrupted, "that she probably goes right back to her fancy Oakview High and tells them stories about us so they all laugh?"

My face flushed scarlet. "I wouldn't do a thing like that," I said.

"Why not?" Joe asked calmly, looking straight at me. "Some of the kids you tell us about have to be your friends, and yet you don't mind telling stories about them."

"I do not tell stories about my friends!" I said forcefully. "Just people like Krystal who ask to be satirized – which means to be made fun of if you didn't know." I got up.

"I have to go to work," I said. "The slave driver is calling."

I ignored their protests and walked through to the kitchen. There wasn't really much to be done. The dishwasher could have waited until later, and Joe wasn't really busy. I gave him a cold stare.

"I guess it really bugs you when I get attention," I said, banging the plates together as I removed them from the dishwasher.

"It bugs me the *way* you get attention," he said. "And go easy on those plates. We're not made of money, you know."

"What do you mean, the way I get attention?" I asked. "You mean because I can tell funny stories and you can't?"

"I mean because you can get laughs at other people's expense," he said.

"I like that!" I said indignantly. "Who is the one who never misses a chance to put down the country club and my sports car and the way I dress and my boyfriend?"

"I don't make fun of my friends," he said, and turned away from me, *leaving an uneasy silence. Anger began to boil over inside.* Why does he always have to act so superior, as if he's Mr Perfect! He's just jealous because the other kids like me because I'm getting the attention now and nobody's interested in him and his dumb Wendy!

Then, as my anger cooled, I realized Joe was right, I had told the kids at school about the kids at the Heartbreak. I had made Pam laugh about Ashley's latest diet tips and Howard's latest movies. I got sympathy from my lunchtime crowd by describing what a pairi Joe was, and I had joked abut other people – not exactly friends – in the stories I told at the café. I put my hand to my hot cheek. Maybe I wasn't such a nice person after all. Maybe Joe could see that. Maybe that was why he didn't like me.

I started to consider summer with my father more seriously again after that. There was no sense in working with a guy who despised me. I could get a job at a real restaurant, one that served real food to grown-up people who would leave me real dollar bills as tips. The café never made any money anyway. It just survived from evening to evening, with sunny weekends keeping it afloat. In fact, the day after the Krystal incident, I came in to find Joe and his grandfather in an argument about money. Their fighting in itself was not unusual. They often fought, with Mr Garbarini doing a lot of yelling and thumping and Joe taking no notice. But tonight, as soon as I walked in the door, Mr Garbarini got me involved.

"You know what this crummy kid say?" he demanded, waving his arms at me. "He say my café stink!"

"I did not," Joe said sulkily. "I only told him that the best thing to do would be to sell and get out because he can't afford to keep this place running the way he operates it."

Mr Garbarini waved his arms again. "Same thing as saying my café stink," he said.

"You can't run a business by letting kids sit around all night and just buy one soda," Joe said.

"So what you want I should do, throw them out? Where else would they go?" his grandfather demanded.

Joe sighed. "I'm not saying you should throw them out, but the café's just not making enough profit to keep going. You're wasting everyone's time by having us work here."

Mr Garbarini turned to me. "The landlord want to raise our rent again," he said in an angry tone. "What do you think we should do?"

I looked from Joe's cold stare to Mr Garbarini's animated face and decided that the best thing would be to keep my mouth shut.

"Me? I don't really know," I said.

"She doesn't care either way," Joe said. "What's it to her if the place closes?"

"Of course I care," I said, feeling that same ready-to- explode anger that Joe always brought out in me. "I know a lot of kids depend on this place, but you have to attract other customers if you want to make a profit. You have to think of getting in other people, maybe doing a lunchtime trade."

"She's right," Mr Garbarini said, thumping his fist down so violently that I jumped. "You think we should open for lunch – get in some of those fancy car people?"

"Not the way the place is now," I said, then almost bit my tongue as soon as it was out.

"What's wrong with my place?" Mr Garbarini demanded.

"It's ... well look at it," I said hesitantly. "It needs upgrading if you want to attract people other than kids."

"Upgrading?" Mr Garbarini savoured the word. "What you think we should do, eh?"

"She wants you to hire an interior decorator, Poppa," Joe said before I could answer, "and put in lots of mirrors and baskets and jungles of plants."

"Why would I want to do that?" the old man demanded. "If I wanted to run a nursery, I'd run a nursery! What do plants have to do with food?"

"They're in right now," Joe said with a sideways look at me. "In all the fancy restaurants you have to fight your way to a table through a jungle."

"Sounds pretty stupid to me," Mr Garbarini said. "And expensive. Plants belong outside in the garden. Tables and chairs belong in a café."

"I think you can make this place look better without spending much," I said quickly before Joe could get another word in.

"Maybe paint the inside, put in some bright tablecloths and

have just a couple of plants in those bare corners. You could upgrade the menu, too, if you want more people to eat here."

"What's wrong with my menu?" Mr Garbarini asked.

"Well," I began, inspiration coming as I talked, "I've had people ask me for salads, and we don't really serve them. All our food is unhealthy. Maybe we should offer a couple of low-cal items on the menu, maybe some fish like those places on the beach. After all, people come down to the beach to eat fish, don't they?"

"Hey, that's not such a bad idea," Mr Garbarini said, giving another of his famous thumps. "You know what I think? I think this young lady's got brains."

"Sure, it's great to talk," Joe said, looking at me with his usual challenging grin, "but who's going to do all this? Who knows how to cook the fish? Who's got time to clean and fillet and do all those things?"

"I don't mind looking into it," I said. "They serve a lot of sauteed calamari at La Lantema. That's good for you and low cal and it doesn't have bones. We could start off with that."

"Good idea," Mr Garbarini said again. "You go ahead, try the calamari and we see if it works. Only don't turn my place into a jungle, you understand?"

"Okay," I said happily, "but I'll try and come up with some ideas for you to make this place look great!"

"Hey, Joe, how come you never come up with ideas to make this place look better?" his grandfather asked.

Joe frowned at me. "Maybe I've been around too long," he said. "I don't have the interest."

I realized afterwards that I was probably committing myself to staying on for a while, but, for the first time since I'd started working, I was excited about doing something really useful. I pictured the café by the time I'd finished with it. All those women in their BMWs would pull up outside.

"Let's go in for lunch," one would say. "I hear they do a fantastic sauteed calamari."

"But my dear, it looks so ordinary," her friend would say.

"Ah, that's just from the outside. You'll be surprised how charming it is inside ..."

I closed my eyes and saw the pink walls and matching tablecloths, the baskets of ferns hanging from the ceiling, the warm glow of pink-shaded lamps, the jukebox playing Italian love songs instead of the usual rock. And when it was a success, even Joe would have to admit that I wasn't such a loser after all. Then I realized something else! My month was almost up. Not only had Joe not made me quit, but I was going to get the last laugh. Suddenly I felt pretty good!

Chapter Thirteen

I decided to get going on the new menu right away, before Mr Garbarini could change his mind. When I saw one of the fishermen who lived down the block walking by the café, I ran out and asked if he could get me some calamari.

"Sure," he said, "how many pounds do you want?"

"Not too many to start with," I said. "We want to introduce it gradually. But if it takes off, I'll want a steady supply."

"Okay, I'll bring you a bucket tomorrow," he said.

At home that night I found two recipes for sauteed calamari in my mother's cookbook. I also took down our big Boston fern, which was hanging in the living room. My mother was always complaining that it was too big for such a small room and that it shed dead leaves all over the floor, so I was sure she wouldn't miss it. Not that she was around to ask. She was always either at class or at some cultural event, and when she was home she was usually sitting at the kitchen counter surrounded by books, muttering to herself. In fact, she only noticed I existed about once a week, and that was usually when she wanted the place cleaned before Norman came over. I noticed he was coming over for more than art history these days. By that I mean that they went to an Indonesian Gamelan Orchestra concert together, and also to an experimental theatre production of *King Lear*. I couldn't see what she saw in him. He was so super wishy-washy and nondescript that I still had my suspicions he was a would-be axe murderer. I watched the way he waved his knife about at dinner, wondering if this was a sign of mental instability or just that he was nervous around my mother.

I got to the Heartbreak early the next day, having stopped on the way to buy garlic, green onions, peppers, and some alfalfa sprouts to add to the burgers. I decided that since we were going health conscious, it was about time the kids got some vitamin C. Ashley, especially, seemed to have no green vegetables in her diet, and I thought she'd hardly notice she was being given healthy food if I slipped some sprouts in between the patty and the pickles. I opened the door and stood there, taking in the café's quiet sleepiness and the lingering French-fry smell. Then I went back to get my plant from the car and hung it in the corner, above the booth. It looked great there and made the corner seem cosier. I was sure that even Mr Garbarini wouldn't object to one innocent Boston fern.

I had just finished unloading my vegetables into the fridge when there was a tap at the back door. My fisherman friend stood there with a bucket in his hands. "Here," he said.

I looked into it. It was full to the brim with slimy, flabby tentacles and hundreds of little fishy eyes stared up at me. I jumped back, my heart beating a mile a minute. "What is that stuff?" 1 asked, looking down with repulsion.

"You asked me to get you some calamari?" he said, looking surprised at my reaction.

"That's calamari?" I asked, turning away with a shudder. The only calamari I'd ever seen was nice white rings of seafood with no bones in them. I had no idea they started off as slimy, creepy things with eyes and tentacles.

"They will be when you cook them," the man said, grinning at me. "Right now they're just a bucket of squid."

"Squid? You mean the same things that wrap their arms round boats and crush them?"

"When they grow up," the fisherman said, chuckling at my stupidity. "These are babies – tender to eat. You know how to clean them?"

"No, I don't."

"It's simple really." He picked one up. "You just cut off the arms, pull back the mantle – like this. Then you cut it into circles. Okay."

"I guess so," I said. "Thank you." I paid for the squid, figuring I could get Mr Garbarini to pay me back later.

I carried the bucket through into the kitchen, holding it well away from me in case any of the squid weren't really dead and one started to climb up the handle. I put the bucket on the kitchen floor and looked at it for a long while. Then I tried to pick up one of the squid, but dropped it again hurriedly. I had never touched anything so gross in my entire life! I knew right then that there was no way I could ever cut up even one squid, let alone a whole bucketful.

I could just tell Mr Garbarini that calamari weren't in season, I thought. I'd carry the bucket down to the beach and throw them back into the ocean and nobody would ever know!

I glanced at my watch. There was just time to make it down to the ocean and back before Joe or his grandfather showed up. I grabbed the bucket again and slunk down Main Street, getting funny looks from the fashionable ladies and praying that I didn't run into anybody I knew. At the end of the street, I climbed down on to the rocks at one end of the beach and worked around tide-pools until I was close to the ocean. A seagull swooped down, landing on a big rock and eyeing me with interest. I shook some squid from the bucket and watched as he swooped to snatch it up. Others joined him, at first just a few, and it was fun to watch them fight over the squid. I tipped out more and pretty soon a whole sky full of seagulls was converging on me, shrieking and snapping as they tried to get to the fish.

Suddenly it wasn't fun any more. It was eerie and threatening, like something out of *The Birds*. I had a funny feeling that they might start trying to eat me as soon as the squid was gone. I tried to back away unnoticed while they were still eating and fighting – and stepped straight into the nearest tidepool!

One minute I was standing on firm rock, the next I was up to my thighs in cold water. I turned round, praying that no one had seen me, and groaned. There was Joe, sitting on the seawall, watching me.

"What exactly are you doing?" he called.

"I'm fading my jeans," I replied coolly. "Salt water is supposed to be the best thing for that."

"With the person still wearing them?" he asked, a triumphant grin spreading across his face.

"So they'll shrink to fit," I said. I tried to climb out gracefully, but the sides of the pool were steep and covered in seaweed. I slid back in.

Anger began to mix with embarrassment. "Well, don't just stand there," I shouted. "Can't you see I'm trying to get out?"

"You want me to help you?" he asked, not moving.

"Of course I want you to help me."

"I didn't realize," he said, sliding down from the wall and landing, catlike, on the sand. "Usually it's only heroic types like your friend the android who rescue maidens in distress. We blue-collar louts aren't very good at it." He took my hand and yanked me out of the pool with one fluid movement. I stood shivering on the sand.

"What were you doing here, anyway?" he asked. "Are you trying to save us money by catching fish?"

He looked into the bucket. One or two squid were still stuck on the bottom. "These are squid," he said. "Don't tell me you caught those in a tidepool – they're deep-water fish."

"I didn't catch them," I said, shivering in the chill wind as my sodden jeans clung to my legs. "I was throwing them back, but then the seagulls came."

"Why?" he asked. "What were you throwing them back for? I thought you were planning to serve them."

"I was," I said. "But when it came time to clean them, they were so yucky that I couldn't do it. I had no idea calamari started off as gross things like this."

I was sure he'd understand and laugh at me for being so squeamish.

Instead the smile faded from his face. "What a waste of good fish," he said.

"Don't worry, I paid for them," I said frostily.

"That's not the point," he said. "You could have asked for help cleaning them. The point is that you wasted good food. Half the world's starving, you know."

"So would you feel better if I wrapped up these last two and sent them to Ethiopia?" I asked, feeling my temper ready to explode at any moment.'

"I want you to be aware," Joe said coolly, starting to head back up the beach. "You're almost out of high school, and I don't think it's crossed your mind once that there are other people in the world besides you."

"You always have to act so superior, don't you?" I said, striding out to catch up with him. "As if you are Mr Perfect and everyone else is nothing. Well, for your information, you have plenty of faults, too! I don't notice you selling your bike to feed the hungry. In fact, I don't notice you thinking about anyone except yourself either."

"That's because you know nothing about me," he said. "I know that you are the most conceited, smug, infuriating boy in the world," I said. "And if I never had to see you again, it would be fine with me!"

I scrambled up the seawall, skinning a toe but determined not to ask him for help. He looked back at me. "Oh, Debbie," he said sweetly.

"Yes?" Maybe he'd realized he'd been behaving like a jerk and was about to apologize.

"You left the bucket down on the rock," he said in a sugary tone. "You'd better get it before the tide washes it away."

I hate him! I hate him! I muttered to myself as I climbed back down to get the bucket. *From now on I'm never going to speak to him again. I'm going to pretend he doesn't exist!*

Chapter Fourteen

The trouble with pretending Joe didn't exist was that he was right there, all evening, bugging me. He could see he had gotten the better of me over the squid incident, and he was making the most of it. I seriously think he was convinced he could make me burst into tears and rush out of there sobbing, that I'd never come back and then he'd win his crummy bet. But it was the knowledge that there were still three more days until the month was up (Joe said it wouldn't be a month until Saturday because my first day was a Saturday) that kept me from losing my temper and stalking out. He was not going to win. It wasn't easy though. All night I put on a calm face and pretended I didn't hear any of his funny remarks. But even so, everything seemed to be going his way. Every single thing I did gave him another chance to make me look like a fool.

I didn't mention the plant I had hung in the corner – after all, one of my ideas had already failed. If nobody commented favourably on it, I was going to put it back in the car and sneak it home again. I didn't think I felt strongly enough to risk having Mr Garbarini yell at me that he didn't want his café turned into a jungle. But since I'd bought all the vegetables, I didn't want to waste them, so after the busy period I started putting sprouts in the burgers – just to see what people thought.

One by one the regulars had drifted in and joined Ashley at the table in the corner. None of them said a thing about my plant, so I silently admitted to myself that it was not a wild success.

Howard arrived, babbling excitedly about the movie he'd just seen. "*Creepers*, it's called. It's a classic," he shouted in my ear. I stood there defenceless, my arms full of plates. "You have seen it, haven't you?"

"'Fraid not," I said. "Now please, let me put these orders down before I drop them."

I pushed past him and set the plates down on the table. Howard followed, one pace behind and breathing hotly down my neck. "Then how about I come over to your place and watch it? You have a VCR, don't you? Real cosy – just the two of us? I'll protect you if you get scared." And he gave me what he thought was his sexy smile.

"I don't think it sounds like my sort of movie, Howard," I said tactfully. "Besides, my mother studies in the evening."

"Your mother studies? Is she in school or something?" Ashley asked, confused as always when anything in life was out of the ordinary.

"Yeah, she's just finishing high school," Joe said, coming up behind me with the fries he had just cooked. "She's the first in the family to learn to read and write."

"No kidding?" Ashley asked. She looked at me with pity. "I had no idea you couldn't read and write."

"She masks it very well," Joe said, giving the crowd a wink, "but you'll notice she doesn't always get the orders straight because she can't write them down."

"Will you guys shut up!" Art said, slipping an arm round my waist. "Just stop teasing for once. You know very well she's smarter than any of us, except Howard maybe."

"Howard, are you supposed to be smart?" Terry asked, taking the pressure off me. I was glad. After falling into a tidepool and facing a bucket full of squid, I wasn't exactly full of smart answers.

Howard blinked through his glasses. "I have an IQ of one

fifty," he said, "which, I understand, is supposed to be genius level."

"So that's why you act so weird, Howard," Art said with a grin. "All geniuses are supposed to be crazy, aren't they?"

"There's nothing weird about me," Howard said, looking offended. "Just because I happen to have a passion for science fiction . . . I don't think you're weird because you have a passion for surfing!"

"That's because surfing's normal," Art said, reaching across to take one of Ashley's French fries.

"Buy your own fries for once," she said, slapping his wrist.

"Just trying to help you stick to your diet," he said, beaming at her.

"I'm on the potato diet this week," she said. "I can eat as many fries as I want to."

"So did any of you see the movie?" Howard asked, squeezing himself into the booth beside Ashley.

"What movie, Howard?" Art asked with a sigh.

"On TV last night, on the late, late show."

"My mom makes me go to bed before the late, late show," Art said, with a good-little-boy look on his face.

"You really missed a great one this time," Howard said excitedly. "Creepers!"

"What?" everyone else asked in unison.

"Creepers!" Howard said again. "It's about these mutant plants from outer space. They start out a little tiny green shoots, and they grow into giant creepers that come in through windows and wrap round people's necks and strangle them and then suck their blood out."

"Eeeuwwww!" Ashley said, putting down her French fry.

"It was the best," Howard went on, blinking excitedly through his glasses and looking at us all one after the other. I think he was convinced he'd win us all over to his movies if he looked excited enough – like a game-show contestant!

"Everything's normal to start with, and then you see all these tiny little green shoots. They start showing up everywhere, just like grass only thinner, and they start to grow and grow until—"

Ashley had just picked up her hamburger, and when she took a bite, she noticed a strange taste and looked down at it.

"Ahhhhhh!" She gave a strangled scream, half choking because her mouth was full of burger. "The shoots! The shoots!" she managed to say, waving her burger at us.

I started to laugh. "It's all right, Ashley," I said. "They're only—"

I could have calmed her easily at this stage, and everything would have been fine, but then she leaned back. The plant I had hung behind her head in the corner was just slightly too long. A tendril brushed against her neck. She looked round and found herself staring at a strand of fern. This time her scream was not strangled. "They're here? Creepers!" She yelled hysterically, making the people at the other tables get nervously to their feet and begin looking round to see which way to run.

I was laughing loudly by this time. It was all so funny. Then I noticed no one else was laughing with me. They had taken the bun off Ashley's hamburger and were all staring at it.

"Someone played a joke on you, Ashley," Terry was saying. "Some bozo put grass in your burger."

The others examined the burger with interest. "Not me, I swear," Art said.

"I put it in," I said, and felt the whole group turn round to look at me. "And it's not grass, Ashley, they're sprouts."

"What?"

"Alfalfa sprouts," I said. "They're good for you."

"What are alfalfa sprouts?" Ashley asked, poking her burger suspiciously.

"A kind of grass," Joe answered before I could.

"You put grass in my burger," Ashley said accusingly, her big eyes turned on me. "I thought you liked me, Debbie."

"Ashley, it's not grass. It's a green plant that's very high in vitamins. I put them in to make your diet more healthy."

"They taste like grass," Ashley said, "and I don't want it." She pushed the burger to one side. "I'm not eating it, Joe."

Joe got up from his perch on the back of Art's bench. "I'll have Debbie cook you a fresh one, okay?" he said.

The way he looked at me was a clear command to get back into the kitchen. My cheeks burning, I walked ahead of him. As soon as we were in there, he shut the door and came up right behind me.

"I hope you've learned your lesson," he said, looking at me coldly.

"Joe, I was just trying to help upgrade this place," I said. "I don't see any harm in a few sprouts on the burgers and a plant in the corner ..."

"Oh, no," he said, his voice laden with sarcasm. "You've only nearly scared off our best customers and caused a panic," he said.

"Your grandfather wanted to make this place a little more upscale, remember? I was trying to help!"

"To get in new lunchtime customers, not scare away our regulars, and certainly not without checking with us first! You've already wasted a bucket of calamari today. How many sprouts did you buy without asking?"

"I was only trying to help!" I defended.

"You were trying to turn this place into something it's not," he said angrily. "It's not one of your yuppie, upscale, trendy restaurants. It's an ordinary café for kids, and that's why they come here. They don't want sprouts in their burgers or plants dangling over their heads. They don't even want calamari." He took out a plate and banged it down on the counter. "Just face it," he said. "You don't belong here and you never will. I thought you were getting over your snobbiness, but in your heart you still look down on us!"

"That is not true," I said. I was feeling close to tears, but there was no way I was going to cry in front of Joe Garbarini.

"It is, too," he said. "Why don't you quit and find somewhere to work where they'll appreciate your creative cooking and your plants in the corner?"

"So you can win your bet?" I asked, my spunkiness returning. I saw his face fall, and I managed a grin. "Ah, you thought I'd forgotten about that, didn't you? Fat chance. That was a nice last-ditch try, but the month's almost over, and as you can see, I'm not going anywhere! There's nothing you can do to make me quit, because I'm as tough as you, Joe Garbarini. So you'd better just admit you've lost."

"What if I set my pet squid on you?" he asked, and there was just the flicker of a smile as he went out to join the others.

The evening seemed to go on for ever and ever. Although I tried to explain myself to Ashley and the others, I could feel the coldness between us, as if I had gone back to being the strange outsider again. Ashley was still all shaken up over her fright and had to have an extra large Chocolate Madness to calm her down. Joe and I did not say a word to each other. I avoided him, leaving the kitchen pointedly when he came in. He wanted this place to fail, I thought. He didn't care if it made a profit or not – he'd rather have the café shut down and be free. Otherwise he'd be able to see that I was trying to help. He's never done anything to attract more customers. He didn't even care that they ate junk food all the time! I was really trying to help, and all he could do was criticize!

Just before closing time, I went to change out of my uniform. He could clean up without me for once. Let him see how useful

I really was around there. "I'm going home," I said. "I'm sure you'll manage fantastically without me, seeing how you know everything and I know nothing!"

I went out, slamming the door, climbed into my car, and roared off into the night. I was about halfway up the canyon when my car gave a cough, a splutter, and died on me. I pulled over off the road and tried to start it again. It sighed, coughed, and was silent again. Then I noticed that the gas gauge was on empty, and I remembered that I'd planned to get gas on my way to work, but I'd been so excited about buying all the vegetables that I'd forgotten all about it. So now I was alone in a dark canyon with the nearest gas station a mile in either direction.

I sat in the car wondering what to do next, trying to fight back the panic that was threatening to overtake me. *Okay, keep calm!* I told myself. *There is nothing to worry about. Just walk to the nearest phone and call Mom, and she'll come and get you. Right!*

Right, I answered myself shakily, while a little voice whispered that the nearest phone was a long dark walk down a deserted canyon at eleven o'clock at night. Maybe I should just sit in my car until morning, I thought. Maybe I should sit in my car until my mother got worried and sent out the police looking for me.

That last thought made me relax. The police! They drove up and down the canyon all the time. I'd wait until a police car came past. A police car would surely stop for a car parked in the darkness like this.

I made sure both doors were locked and wished for once that I had a regular car and not a convertible. Anyone with a sharp knife could cut his way through the top of this car! I was very conscious of the complete silence. No cars passed. When I rolled down the window, I could hear the wind rustling dry branches and the chirping of enough night insects and frogs to make it sound like the background for a jungle movie. I might have been in the middle of the Amazon instead of a mile from the lights of civilization.

I began to feel very cold. The chilly night air had managed to find its way in through the seams in the canvas. It felt as if I'd been sitting there for hours. Why hadn't any cars come by? Then, finally, I heard a noise – the roar of an approaching engine coming round the bend. *Let it be a police car,* I prayed.

The interior of my car was lit by a headlight. I heard the engine slow to a stop. Bright light was shining in my rear window, almost blinding me. I turned round, but I could see nothing. If it was a police car, it sure didn't have any red or blue lights on.

What if it was a stranger? I thought. What should I do if a strange man came to the window? I wouldn't unlock the door, that's for sure. I'd yell to him to tell the closest gas station.

A large dark shape appeared, throwing a shadow right up the canyon. A tall figure towered over me, then leaned towards the window. It was all I could do not to scream. The figure tapped on the glass, and I looked up to see Joe's face a few inches from mine.

"What happened?" he yelled through the window.

I wound down the window.

"Don't tell me this miracle of German engineering just broke down?" he asked.

"Break down?" I asked, trying to keep my voice from showing any panic. "Of course not. I just stopped to admire the view."

"The view?" He gave me a suspicious look. "It's dark out there, in case you hadn't noticed." He paused. "Are you sure you don't need a ride?"

"A ride?" I asked.

"Yeah, a ride," he said impatiently. "Do you need a ride up to a gas station or something?"

A war was going on inside my head, with the rational part telling me that I needed to get out of this canyon right now and that Joe's bike would be as good a way as any, while the irrational part of me argued that I'd never live it down if Joe had to rescue me. Besides, what if someone I knew saw me on the back of Joe's bike?

"It's okay," I said. "I'm just fine, thanks."

He continued to look at me. "Did anyone ever tell you you were stubborn as a mule?" he asked. "And dumb, too."

"Will you just go?" I said. "I told you I'd be fine. I only stopped for a few minutes. I'll be on my way again in a minute."

He stood up again, towering over the car so that I could only see the zipper on his leather jacket.

"Suit yourself," he said. "It's a long dark walk up the hill."

He began to walk away. Reason began to overtake my pride. I did not want to be left here. Being rescued on the back of Joe's bike with my hair every which way and my pride crushed was better than not being rescued at all. I opened the door of the car. "All right, Joe, you win ..." I began, when I heard his engine rev up, and he roared past me up the hill.

Chapter Fifteen

I can't describe how bad I felt as I watched Joe's taillight snake up the canyon and then disappear round a bend. I called myself all kinds of dumb names, but that didn't make me feel any better. If only he were a normal person, I argued with myself. If only he would treat me like a normal person, of course I would have ridden with him. But look how he'd behaved over the squid! Look how he'd put me down over those sprouts! He'd be getting laughs about this at the café for weeks to come!

And now? a little voice inside whispered. Wouldn't he have an equally good story to tell now? Not so funny, maybe, but more dramatic – about the girl who was so stubborn and so stupid that she wouldn't accept a ride and got herself raped or murdered instead.

I shivered and double-checked that both doors were locked. Not that that was much good, because almost anyone could just wrestle off the top of this little car. I pictured myself escaping as he tore the top off, running blindly down the canyon while his heavy footsteps gained on me. Would Joe be even a little sorry when he heard they'd found my body in the morning? Would he come to see me, laid out in a little white coffin, and bend to kiss my cold cheek and murmur, "If only I'd been nicer to her, this would never have happened"?

"Of course he wouldn't," I muttered. He'd say I was a stupid girl who had got what she deserved.

I had almost decided I was safer running back down the canyon than sitting as a target in my car when the police car arrived.

"Boy, am I glad to see you," I said as the policeman walked up to my window. "I thought no more patrols would be driving down this road tonight and I'd be stuck here."

The policeman smiled, a broad, fatherly smile. "You have a friend to thank," he said. "Young man called us a few minutes back. He said you were stuck in the canyon, and he was in too much of a hurry to stop and help you!"

It was with a mixture of gratitude and hatred that I climbed out of my car and accepted a ride in the police car. All the nearby gas stations were closed, so the policeman insisted on driving me all the way home. I could come back and get my car in the morning. It was almost midnight by the time we pulled up outside the condo, and I wished more and more that I'd accepted Joe's offer of a ride. I'd rather have arrived on a bike, looking windblown and a mess, than have the old woman in curlers next door see me get out of a police car, which was what happened. I don't know if she watched at her window, but the moment the car stopped, she opened her front door and stood there, curlers and all, watching me as I got out of the car and went to our front door. I nearly died of embarrassment. *She probably thinks I got busted for something,* I thought in horror.

"Well, thanks very much for the ride. I'm glad you rescued me when my car broke down. It was very dumb of me to run out of gas!" I said in my loudest voice, hoping the curler lady and anyone else who wais listening would hear.

The noise brought my mother to the front door. Dressed in her robe, with cream on her face, she looked just as bad as the curler lady.

"What's happened, Deborah? Are you all right?" She called and started to come down the front path.

I was already embarrassed enough to last a lifetime. Sprinting towards her, I steered her back into the house.

"Hi, Mom, I'm just fine. My car broke down, that's all," I said, closing the door firmly behind us. "A policeman brought me home."

She turned to face me. "I was worried sick about you," she said. "It's so late ... I didn't know what to think."

"I ran out of gas, that's all," I said. "No big deal."

"No big deal?" she asked, her voice rising to a squeak. "That was a very irresponsible thing to do. You honestly don't deserve a car if you can't look after it. Do you realize what could have happened to you on a lonely road at midnight?"

"I didn't run out of gas on purpose," I said, walking down the hall ahead of her, "and I said I was sorry. I'm safely home now so everything's okay, and we can both go to bed."

"It's past midnight," my mother said, not wanting to let me get away. "And on a school night, too."

I thought she was concerned about my not getting enough sleep. "Don't worry. I don't have to work tomorrow," I said, but she leaped on me.

" *You* don't have to work tomorrow? Did it ever occur to you that I have to get enough sleep, too? I wanted to go to bed by ten tonight, because I've got my first midterm in two days. I've been studying all evening, and I have to study all of tomorrow."

I turned to face her. "Hey, I just said I was sorry, Mom," I said. "How much more sorry do you want me to be? If we had a fireplace, I'd find some sackcloth and ashes for you. I could grovel! I could get down on my knees and kiss your feet. Would that make you feel better?"

I saw the ghost of a smile flicker across her lips. "Just go to bed," she said, giving me a gentle push.

Once in bed, I had a hard time getting to sleep. I was cold all over. I curled into a tight little ball and tucked my feet under my nightgown, but I was still shivering. I suppose it might have been delayed shock. I kept thinking about the other time in my life that I got lost. It was back in third grade. Another Brownie and I got separated from the troup on a hike, and we didn't get back to the trailhead until after dark. We were both pretty scared, but my parents were there, waiting to scoop me up into their arms, whisking me home and tucking me into my bed after some hot cocoa. I really wanted that cocoa now. I guess what I really wanted was a parent who was more concerned about me getting lost than she was about some dumb test she had to take.

The next morning I was tired and grouchy. I was almost late for school because I had to ride with my mother to pick up my stranded car, and I didn't have time to wash my hair, which made me feel icky and tense. To make matters worse, Grant was waiting for me in the parking lot.

"Where were you last night?" he asked. "I called several times."

"Working," I muttered. "I had to work late." I wasn't going to tell Grant about running out of gas. I had a feeling I might get another lecture about all the terrible things that could have happened to me.

Grant slipped an arm around my shoulder. "Don't worry, Cinderella," he said, looking down at me tenderly, "Prince Charming is here to whisk you away from all that drudgery."

"He is?" I asked cautiously.

"I found you another job," he said, beaming at me. "It's just right for you, Debbie. You'll love it!"

"What is it?" I asked, still cautiously.

"At the pro shop at the club," he said, as if he had produced a rabbit out of a hat for me. "You'd like that, wouldn't you? Selling equipment, signing out carts, taking reservations for courts. Right up your alley, isn't it?"

"The pro shop?" I asked suspiciously. I was suspicious because I knew that Pam had looked into getting a job there the summer before, and they'd said there was only enough work for one person. "Don't they still have that Austrian woman?"

"Sure they do," Grant said easily, "but she could use some help. They'll pay six dollars an hour, and you can pick you own hours. Work as much as you like."

"I don't understand," I said, thinking it would be sort of nice to have an easy job that paid six dollars an hour. Then I began to understand. A connection was forming in my head. "Isn't your uncle still president of the club?" I asked.

Grant's face reddened. "Of course," he said.

"And you asked him to get me this job?"

"I mentioned it to him, of course," he said off-handedly. I could almost hear the conversation: Grant describing to his uncle how poor Debbie had come down in the world and had to live in a condo and scrub floors ... the tension of the previous night stretched to the snapping point. "You can tell your uncle I don't want his nonexistent job," I said angrily.

Grant looked confused. "What do you mean?"

"You know very well what I mean, Grant," I said. We were approaching the main entrance to school, and Grant looked around in embarrassment because my voice carried across the courtyard. "There is no real job, is there? You asked your uncle to help me out, right? You know as well as I do that it doesn't take two people to book tennis lessons and sell sweatbands."

Grant grabbed me by the arm, pulling me aside so that we were both not swept into the stream of students. "It has to be better than scrubbing floors in a cheap café!" he said. "Anything is better than that."

"At least it's a real job, where I'm needed," I said.

"What do you see yourself as, a saint? Working among the lowlife of town?" he asked.

"I tell you one thing I'm not," I yelled. "I'm not a charity case. I don't need to be helped by having strings pulled for me. I don't need your uncle to make up a job for me."

Grant looked as if I'd slapped him across the face. "I was only trying to help, Debbie," he said stiffly.

"If you really want to help me then stop interfering in my life!" I said.

He looked straight at me. "Maybe I should stay out of your life altogether," he said evenly. "Maybe we just aren't right for each other any more."

"If that's the way you feel," I said shakily. "Maybe you're right."

The bell rang for first period, and we both walked stiffly in opposite directions, like two sleepwalkers through the crowd.

Chapter Sixteen

It's been my experience that days that start off badly just get worse. This one certainly did! I hadn't read the assigned book in English and Mr Hurwitz called me up in front of the class to give my impression of the main characters. I might as well have given my impression of Mickey Mouse and Donald Duck. He let me stammer on for five minutes before he said curtly, "I don't think you've bothered to read the book, have you, Debbie?" then there was a test in chemistry, full of problems that just didn't make sense, and Pam was not even available at lunchtime, because she had a Debate Club meeting. It seemed that all my friends were in the Debate Club and I wandered round the schoolyard alone, feeling empty and scared and sorry for myself.

It's true, I thought miserably. *I don't belong anywhere any more.*

I refused to think about Grant. I kept him shut firmly away in a little compartment at the back of my mind. I wouldn't even listen to the nagging voice that kept whispering that I'd lost my first and only real boyfriend ...

I arrived home from school to find my mother surrounded by notes and reference books, having taken over the whole kitchen table. "Michelangelo, fourteen seventy-five to fifteen ..." she was muttering as I came in. She opened a book and slammed it shut again. "Dammit," she said, acknowledging my presence with a nod, "I'll never get these dates straight."

"Want me to test you?" I asked.

"It's no good testing me if I know I don't know the material, is it?" she asked sharply.

"I'll make dinner tonight," I said, "so you can study."

"Did you bring the chicken?" she asked, already poring through another book.

"Chicken? What chicken?"

"I asked you to get a chicken for dinner," she said, looking up and peering at me over her glasses. "Don't tell me you forgot."

"I could hardly forget if you never told me in the first place, could I?" I said.

"I distinctly remember," my mother said. "When I left you with your car I told you we needed a chicken for dinner tonight."

"Y-yes," I said hesitantly. "You did say something about a chicken, but I didn't think you were asking me to get one."

"You might have realized I don't have time," she snapped, running her hands through her hair. "I have all this to get through!"

"Come on, Mom, it can't be that bad," I said, putting a hand awkwardly on her shoulder. "It's only Shoreline College, not Yale. All the flakes from school go there. You have to be smarter than they are!"

She glared at me angrily. "I might be smarter," she said, "but unlike me, they've been to school in the past hundred years." She continued to glare. "You think this whole thing is a big joke, don't you? Middle-aged mother dabbling at being a student because she can't get a job in the real world!"

"I don't think that at all," I said.

"Well, you're not exactly backing me up, are you?" she said, her voice rising dangerously. "You keep me awake half the night, and now you can't even remember to bring home a simple chicken for dinner."

"I'll go get the chicken," I said, with an exaggerated sigh. "I don't suppose it matters that I'm way behind with my homework, too."

"Only because you're spending your entire life at that horrible café!" she yelled.

"Because I suddenly find that I don't have a mother who's prepared to support me any more, even though it's the law," I shouted back.

"What do you think I'm trying to do by going back to college?" she yelled.

"Flaking out, that's what. Having a great time playing at being a kid again and putting all the responsibility on my shoulders!" I screamed. There, I'd said it out loud. "You're not even trying to be a mother any more!"

"Maybe because I'm tired of having a daughter who acts like a spoiled brat," she said, suddenly cold and calm.

I swallowed hard. "Then perhaps I'd better move out, so you can do your own thing, playing at being a college student. We don't seem to need each other any more," I said, trying to sound as calm and icy as she was.

"Don't be stupid," she said. "Where do you think you would go?"

"Dad wants me," I said, feeling a sudden rush of warmth and security as I spoke his name. "Dad likes having me around."

"Your father didn't want either of us around," she said, her voice wavering. "That was why he left. We're just liabilities."

"You, maybe," I said, a little too forcefully. "He wants me. He said so. He said anytime was fine with him, and he doesn't have stupid schedules and rules and he doesn't have a conniption over a stupid chicken!"

I rushed into my room and began throwing clothes into my old duffel bag. I heard my mother behind me saying, "Deborah, don't be so childish!"

"Childish!" I muttered as I kept on stuffing clothes into the bag. "It seems to me that I'm the only one who's not being childish. I'm the only one with a job round here. I'm the only one who's trying to juggle school and work, too. I'm not trying to starve my kid to death because I don't have any time to cook any more." The bag was full. I grabbed my stuffed elephant from the bed and tucked him under one arm. "Well, you don't have to worry about cooking chickens for me any more. I won't be around to get in your way," I said, pushing past her to the front door. She was yelling something after me, but I didn't even stop to listen.

I drove to Dad's house, speeding all the way. I didn't even slow up much when I left the highway and took the narrow road that twisted and turned down into Dad's little town. I could feel the tyres protesting at each bend, but I kept on going until I pulled up outside the pink frosted building. My feet clattered over the ceramic tiles. I took the stairs two at a time. Suddenly I was terrified that he wouldn't be home, that he'd have gone to Los Angeles to sign a contract for a screenplay or even that he was just out walking on the beach. But when I tapped on his door I heard a scuffling inside and Dad called, "Who is it?"

"Dad? It's me, Debbie!" I shouted back through the thick wooden door.

There was more scuffling inside, then the door was opened. Dad's hair was tousled, as if he'd just woken up. My impression that he was still half-asleep was confirmed when he stared at me as if he were trying to decide that it was really me, standing outside his front door.

"Debbie?" he asked cautiously. "What are you doing here? It's not the weekend."

"No, it's Thursday," I said, "but I had to see you."

"The court said you're only supposed to visit on weekends," he said, still cautiously.

"I don't care what it said," I insisted, feeling like I might cry if he left me out on the doorstep a minute longer. "I have to talk to you, Dad. Can I come in?"

"Come in?" he echoed, then seemed to get hold of himself. "Oh, sure, Debbie. Come on in. What's the problem, is something wrong?"

I walked ahead of him into the living room and slumped on to his old lumpy sofa. "It's Mom," I said. "We just had a big fight. I don't think she wants me there any more. She doesn't seem to care about me at all."

He came over and sat beside me. "You know that's not true, honey," he said gently. "Your Mom cares a lot about you. It's just that she's finding it hard to adjust. We all are."

"You seem to be doing fine," I said. "You've adjusted. You're having a great time."

"Not all the time, Debbie," he said. "You just think I've adjusted because you've only seen the good side. You haven't seen all the times I've been overcome with guilt and doubts. Honey, we all have our ups and downs, don't we? You and your Mom are just going through a normal mother-daughter conflict. All teenage girls fight with their mothers. You're just a late bloomer!" And he laughed, as if he's said something funny.

"It wasn't just a normal fight," I said, playing with the fringe on the afghan that covered the sofa. "It was a horrible fight, a major fight. I walked out, Dad. I told 'her I was going to live with you."

"You did what?" his voice sounded sharp. It made me look up from my braided afghan fringe.

"I want to live with you, Dad," I said.

"But you can't do that," he said, a strange look coming into his eyes. "The court said you live with your mother and visit here. We have to abide by that, you know."

"I don't want to abide by that," I said. "Mrs Farbstein said she wanted what was best for me. We could go back and tell her that I've changed my mind and it's best for me to stay here." I looked at him, pleadingly, willing him to smile at me and tell me that he wanted me here more than anything.

Instead he swallowed hard. I saw his Adam's apple moving up and down. "Pumkin, girls belong with their mothers," he said uneasily. "I love to see you, but this isn't the right place for you to live. It's not near a good school, your friends aren't here, and I don't have room for you to live here permanently ..."

"Then let me stay for a while, okay?" I asked. "I don't want to go back to Mom tonight. I can stay here tonight, can't I?"

He cleared his throat. His Adam's apple danced up and down again. "Well, actually ..." he began slowly, "it's not – I mean, I had planned ..." He looked at my face and his own face softened. "I guess you could stay for one night," he said. "I don't suppose anyone would object to that, would they? How about if I come down right now and help you with your things? Or better still, how about if we go out for a cup of coffee together first? I'm dying for a good cup of coffee and I've only got instant in the house."

"Okay, Dad," I said, smiling at him happily. "That would be great. But I have to use your bathroom first. I haven't been since I left school and that was hours ago." I crossed the room and opened the bedroom door before he could say anything. I heard him call, "No, wait a minute, Debbie. Don't go in there. It's a complete mess in there!"

I looked back and laughed. "You should see my room if you want to see a mess," I said. "Nothing would faze me—"

But something did. I opened the bathroom door and found myself staring at a person who was trying to hide in the shower. She had lots of wavy blonde hair, and she didn't look a whole lot older than me. I took in her tousled hair, and blouse, which was buttoned all wrong. My father appeared behind us before I could say a word.

"Er, Debbbie, this is Susan," he said in a funny voice. "She's a neighbour. She just popped in to borrow—"

"A cup of sugar?" I asked, staring at Susan, whose face was now bright pink.

"Actually, she wanted to borrow my shower," my father said.

A bright bubble of anger was forming in my head. "Where was she going to take it?" I asked sweetly.

My father cleared his throat. "What I mean is, her shower broke and I said she could use mine."

"That's right, my shower broke. I keep telling the maintenance man he should fix it," the girl said. She had a silly, high-pitched voice, and she giggled afterwards.

I looked at both of them and began to back out of the bathroom. "Come on, Dad, I'm not two years old any more," I said. I was trying to keep my voice even, but I could hear myself babbling on as I fought with my embarrassment and anger. "You don't have to protect me. If you want to fool around, I guess that's up to you. Only don't lie to me, okay? I'm sick of people who lie to me and treat me like I don't matter!"

"Calm down, Debbie, do you want the whole building to hear?" my father said, moving towards me. He reached out to grab my shoulder, but I shook his hand off. "I'm calm," I went on. "I'm very calm. Why shouldn't I be calm? Just because my father ... my own father ..."

"Debbie," he said, in his reasonable lawyer's voice. "Debbie, let's try to be adult, shall we?"

"Adult?" I shrieked. "I like that. That's pretty funny." I kept on going across his living room. I opened the front door. "Oh, well, 'bye Dad. Gotta go. Nice seeing you again. Maybe we can have coffee some time in the next couple of years, if you can spare the time, that is."

I heard him call, "Debbie, wait!" but I clattered all the way down those tiled steps and jumped back into my car. I didn't even look in the rearview mirror to see if he had come down after me. I just put my foot on the gas pedal and felt the car leap forward as I roared off.

Chapter Seventeen

I didn't even know where I was going. Instead of driving back up to the highway, I kept going straight, along the narrow coast road. I just put my foot down and drove, as if by itself driving might blot out everything else. The top of my car was down, and the wind tore through my hair, fanning it out behind me. I hadn't noticed what kind of day it was until then, but as I drove up on to a clifftop, I felt the full force of the blustery wind. A few rain-drops spattered on to my head. Still I kept on driving, taking each curve with cold confidence as the road dropped from clifftop down to the beach and then snaked its way up the next bluff and back down again. Driving at shore level, the wind and surf roared in my ears. I tasted sea spray on my lips and felt at one with the power of the wind and the waves. I was alone. The car was my cocoon. If I kept driving far enough and fast enough, I could escape everything!

I kept driving in this almost hypnotized trance, meeting almost no traffic, seeing no one, along the deserted coast highway until I was almost back at Rockley Beach. I drove down to a rocky cove just south of the town. The road crossed an estuary by a narrow bridge. I was just about to drive on to the bridge when a truck came in the opposite direction. It took me a few seconds to reg-ister that there wasn't room for both of us on the bridge. At first, I was all set to try and sneak by the truck. Luckily I came to my senses at the last moment, slammed on the brakes, and came to a stop on the sandy shoulder as the truck roared past me. I was shaking all over as it gradually hit me how close I'd come to killing myself.

I've got to calm down, I said out loud. *I've got to get my head together again before I drive another foot.*

I got out of the car and crossed the road to the beach. It wasn't much of a beach, really – just a little half moon of sand sandwiched between some rocks, over which the surf was breaking. Spray from the waves drifted across the beach like a lace curtain when the wind caught it. I crossed the sand, standing at the edge of the ocean, watching each wave crest and collapse with a boom on to the beach. It was not an ocean from a travel poster today. Only an idiot like Art would be even tempted to think about surfing. The ocean was fierce and destructive and powerful, and I was half-frightened that one of the waves would be bigger than the rest and swallow me up.

I wondered how my parents would feel about that? Would they feel guilt and remorse when they went to identify my body, washed up on a beach somewhere down the coast? Would they hold hands behind my white coffin and whisper, "If only we'd stayed together, just for her sake. If only we'd paid more attention to her and not made her feel unloved and unwanted." I saw them, dressed in smart but simple black, my father in shoes again instead of sandals, following along with the funeral procession. Grant was there, too, and Pam. Joe was at the rear, not wanting to come too close to mourners, but watching, white-faced and tight-lipped, as if he, too, might cry at any moment.

It was a satisfying scene. As I let it play in my head, I reached the edge of the sand and began to scramble up the first of the rock ledges. From there I didn't feel so intimidated by the waves. They weren't crashing down on me. I was looking down on them. I walked closer to the edge and stood for some time, watching the wave pattern, noticing how some waves sent up fountains of spray while others sighed and died over the lowest rocks. I picked my way over seaweed covered shelves, closer to the edge of the ocean. I was close enough to feel spray drift over me. I could see drops of it sparkling like jewels in my hair. It was better to watch waves than think, seriously, about my future.

The waves were making such a noise that I didn't hear, anyone come up behind me until a voice spoke.

"Don't tell me the miracle of German engineering has broken down again. Or are you disposing of more squid?" I spun around to see Joe standing behind me, looking more than ever like a rugged guy from a cigarette advertisement, or maybe an ad for a brand of very masculine cologne: *SEASPRAY – FOR MEN WHO ARE MEN!* His leather jacket was open, and he was wearing a striped T-shirt underneath it. His dark hair was windswept and his cheeks were tanned. He was also the last person in the world that I wanted to see.

"What are you doing here?" I demanded. "Why aren't you at the café?"

"I got out early for good behaviour," he said. "Actually I'm taking a break. It's slow this afternoon and Poppa's in a bad mood."

"Do you spend all your free time sneaking up on people on beaches?" I asked.

"I saw your car," he said. "I was driving past, and I thought you might need rescuing again."

"No, thank you," I said.

"You didn't break down?"

"No."

"That's what you said last time, when I had to get the police to come help you."

I turned away. "Look," I said quietly. "I just want to be alone. Okay?"

"Oh, okay," he said.

There was a pause. I went on watching the ocean. I guess he didn't go because soon he said in a quiet voice, "Look, Debbie, would it help to talk about it?" He put his hand on my shoulder. I was so startled by the contact that I almost jumped. It was the first time he had ever touched me.

I eyed him suspiciously, waiting to see the hint of sarcasm or triumph, waiting for Joe to pounce on Debbie's latest tragedy. But his dark eyes looked at me steadily.

"There's nothing to talk about," I said uneasily. A new, sympathetic Joe was something I found hard to deal with.

"Sometimes things are easier if you talk about them," he said. "Just knowing someone else is willing to listen . . ."

"There's nothing you can do," I said dejectedly. "There's nothing anyone can do. It's all hopeless."

"Are you in some kind of trouble?" he asked, visualizing me, I think, standing on the steps of the Home for Unmarried Mothers.

I shook my head. "Not in the way you're thinking," I said.

"In fact, I'm not the trouble at all. I'm the only normal, sane, responsible person in this whole mess."

A wave crashed on to the rocks below with a giant whoomp, splattering us with spray. Joe took my elbow. "I think you should come down from here," he said. "People are always being swept off these rocks by freak waves."

"So who cares," I said, turning away from him. "I doubt my folks would even come to the funeral. My mother wouldn't want to miss her art history class and my father wouldn't want to leave his tootsie."

"Don't talk dumb," Joe said, putting pressure on my elbow. "Come back from there."

"Just leave me alone, Joe," I said, shaking him off.

"I am not leaving so you can get swept off a rock," he said firmly. "I thought you were more intelligent than that."

"Don't worry," I said. "I'm not considering suicide. I'm just standing and thinking, and no waves will come up this high." As if my words were a challenge, a wave, larger than the rest, came racing over the lower shelves. I turned to move up the rocks, slipped on the seaweed, and went sprawling. I heard Joe yell something, then strong arms grabbed me and I was dragged away like a sack of potatoes, as the wave soaked my legs, then receded.

"Boy, you sure are stubborn," Joe said, panting with the effort. I scrambled to my feet. "Thanks," I said, shivering as the wind plastered my wet jeans to my legs. "I had no idea the waves would come this high."

"That's what all the people who were swept off thought," Joe said, leading me back towards the cliffs, step by step, as if I were a little child. "When you watch the ocean, you know how often there are freak waves. Every ninth wave, they say, is a giant."

"You do a lot of ocean watching?" I asked, amazed. I would have found it easier to believe girl watching or football watching.

"Quite a bit," he said. "I often ride over to this beach when I need to be alone and think. There's nowhere to be alone with my family."

"Maybe we could trade," I said. "I have parents who don't even want to know I exist."

"You wouldn't want to trade," Joe said shortly. "Here, come and sit out of the wind. You're shivering."

He pulled me into a little half cave, carved by the force of water at the base of the cliff. I allowed him to steer me like a puppet, and I sat when he told me to sit. He sat close beside me, and I was conscious of the warmth of his body. "That's better," he said. "What are you doing out here, anyway? It's a little off your normal route, isn't it?"

"I just went to see my father," I said, the whole miserable afternoon coming back in horrible detail. "He lives down in Whitney Cove."

"Is he an artist?" Joe asked, surprised. "I thought he was a lawyer."

"He was," I said bitterly. "He just decided he'd rather be a writer and live a free, creative life. I've just found out what his idea of a free, creative life is. He had a girl there, and she was barely older than me!"

Joe looked at my indignant face, grinned, and then tried to stifle it.

"It's not funny," I said.

"No, of course not," Joe answered, clearing his throat. "But I guess what he does with his life is up to him, isn't it?"

"When you're a parent, aren't you supposed to take care of your kids, not just suddenly pretend they don't exist any more?" I demanded. "Because both my parents seem to be having a ball after they split up. If they'd cared at all about me, they'd have stayed together until I was in college, wouldn't they?"

Joe looked at me, surprised. "So is that what's bugging you, that your parents aren't devoting themselves full-time to you any more?"

The way he put it made me sound like a spoiled little kid. "No!" I said angrily. "Not just that. They don't want me around at all! I walked out on my mother because she started yelling at me because I forgot to buy a chicken. She's always yelling at me and expecting me to do everything while she goes to every concert and play and art exhibit in the world. So I went to see my father. I thought he really wanted me, but it turns out he didn't after all." I was yelling now. Joe put his hand on my arm.

"Hey, cool it," he said. "Maybe you're just going to have to be adult about this."

"Adult?" I shouted, shaking his hand from my arm. "It seems

to me that I'm the only adult I know! That's what both my parents keep saying. 'Act like an adult, Debbie! Be adult about it all!' Well, I've got a mother who's going to school and a dad who's dating twelve-year-olds, and they both keep telling me to act like an adult! It feels as if the whole world's turned upside down!"

Joe just let me yell. Afterwards we sat there for a while, listening to the boom of the surf and the screech of gulls. I drew pictures in the sand beside me.

"Look," he said at last, "I know it's not easy for you, but maybe all you can do is face the fact that nobody's going to spoon-feed you any more. You had it too good before. You had parents who cared about you and looked after you and you were the centre of their little world. Some kids never have that. They have parents who don't notice they exist from day one." He was silent for a while, staring out at the ocean, hugging his knees to him, like a little kid. "Or," he said slowly, "you have parents who think that they own you. That you are someone who has no rights and no life outside the family."

His voice cracked and I looked at him. He was still staring out at the water. "Is that like your family?" I asked cautiously.

He nodded. "I wasn't joking when I said that I've worked in their deli since I was three years old. Every moment of my life when I'm not in school, I'm working for my family. Never time to play ball with the other kids. I tried out for football freshman year in high school. Know what the coach said? He said, 'Garbarini, you could get yourself a scholarship if you work hard. You've got the ability.' But my parents didn't let up. My Mom's been sick and my Dad strained his back, and I had to start missing practices. The coach said I had to choose, but there wasn't any choice, was there?" He looked at me for the first time, and I saw the anger and hopelessness in his eyes. "You know Italian families," he said. "You don't disobey. Everything's for the family! You get disowned if you step out of line!" He laughed, grimly. "Italian mothers are really good at laying guilt trips on their kids. See, they came from the old country with nothing – Grandpa first, then he sent for my father. 'All this will be yours, Joe!' they say, as if I wanted their crummy deli! I can't even go away to college. I'm going to have to fit in part-time courses at Shoreline, while I manage the deli. My Dad keeps talking about Poppa wanting to retire, and how then I can run the café *and* the deli, and all I can see is me stuck for ever and ever."

"What would you like to do?" I asked gently. The wind had blown a strand of dark curly hair across his forehead, making him look very vulnerable.

He shrugged in a typically Italian gesture. "I wouldn't have minded playing football," he said. "Make a few million, retire. I also like to draw, but I've never had a chance to see how good I am. Drawing is not exactly macho, so I don't do it at home."

"I might not be able to go to a good college, either," I said. "I might be joining you at Shoreline. All these years I've worked hard for good grades, and now we might not have the money."

"So life is tough," Joe said.

"But it's not fair!" I blurted out. "It's not fair to me or to you!"

He put his hand back on my arm. "Parents don't owe you anything, you know. They gave you life. The rest is up to you. You'll find out that in the end, the only person you can ever rely on is yourself! If you want to get anywhere, Debbie, you have to take charge of your own life."

A big sob was building at the back of my throat. Tears welled up in my eyes. "But I can't," I said as the sob escaped. "Don't they see that? Don't they see that I'm not grown up yet? I want someone to still take care of me. I'm scared ..."

"Hey," Joe said gently, "come on. It will be okay. You'll see." Then, more insistently, "Oh, no, don't cry. I can't stand it when girls cry." He put his arms round me awkwardly. I tried to stop crying, but it was as if someone had turned on a giant faucet inside me. All the times I'd wanted to cry since the divorce had been rolled into one. I buried my head into his shoulders and sobbed. I felt his arms tighten round me.

"Come on, Debbie," he whispered into my ear. "Don't cry, please. You're going to make me cry, too, and I'll be so embarrassed."

I looked up at his face in surprise and half laughed through my tears. He laughed, too. Then suddenly he was kissing me, tenderly and full on the mouth. Before I knew it, I was kissing him back. The kiss went on for a long time. When we finally broke apart, we stayed there, our arms wrapped round each other, staring at each other incredulously. Slowly Joe let me go. He got to his feet.

"Well, that stopped you crying, anyway," he said with an embarrassed laugh.

I got to my feet, too. "That's the way to do it, I guess," I said shakily, and I laughed, too.

He held me by the arm. "Look, Debbie ..." he began hesitantly.

"I better be going," I said. "I don't want to find myself driving up this road in the dark."

"And I'd better get back to the café," Joe said. "One of us has to keep things running, you know. We don't all get days off."

I started to walk ahead of him, taking giant strides down the rock steps. "Well, see you, Joe," I said, not looking back at him. "Thanks for stopping."

"Anytime," he said. I looked back. His dark eyes held me steadily. "Anytime you run out of gas, I'll be around."

"And anytime the French fryer breaks, down and you burn yourself, I'll be around, too." I quipped back.

We looked at each other for a moment, then both grinned at the same time. Then I went to my car and he went to his bike, and we both drove away in opposite directions.

Chapter Eighteen

I stopped at the deli on the way home and picked up a chicken. When I swung into the parking lot, the first thing I saw was Grant's red Alfa, parked beside the row of garbage cans, with Grant sitting on the hood. He slid off it when he saw me and stood there awkwardly.

"Hi," he said, walking over to me as I got out of the car.

"Hi."

Nervously he pushed his hair back, although it was never out of place. "I've been waiting here quite a while," he said. "Your mother said she didn't know when you'd be back, but I decided to stick around."

"I was out for a drive," I said. "I needed time to think."

He swallowed hard. "I hope I wasn't the one who made you upset," he said. "I've been feeling so bad all day, Debbie."

"I said some pretty mean things to you, too," I answered.

"I was only trying to help, you know."

"I know."

There was a pause while we stood and looked at each other, both waiting for the other to say they were sorry first, I guess. It suddenly struck me as funny, like a scene from a movie in which we both had set lines to speak.

Grant spoke first. "Look, Debbie, I'm sorry," he said. Because it was his movie line, I had to choke back a giggle, but I think he thought I was trying not to cry because he went on. "I should have realized that you've been under enough pressure as it is. I know what you've been through this year, what with the divorce and the move and everything. It can't have been easy to take a job like that."

I looked up at him. "You were trying to control my life for me, Grant," I said finally. "That's what I couldn't handle."

"I realized that, too," he said. "I saw that I'd hurt your pride and that was a dumb thing to do." He smiled suddenly. "I guess that's one of the things I always liked about you, that you're so stubborn," he said. "I admire you for wanting to make your own mistakes."

I shook my head. "You still think the café's a mistake, don't you?" I asked. "You really think that I'm sticking to the job just to be stubborn!"

He took a step towards me. "I just don't think it's the place you're destined for," he said, "but I suppose one job is as good as another until we can wave our Harvard degrees at everyone." He slipped his hands round my waist and pulled me towards him. "Can we make up?" he asked. "I don't want to waste the rest of my senior year without you."

"If you promise not to find me any more jobs watching the grass grow," I said smiling at him.

His arms tightened round me. "You ought to run for Congress," he said. "You'd be the only politician who couldn't be bought."

"No, thanks," I said emphatically. "I don't know much about the future but one thing I know I don't want to be is a politician." I stared at him steadily. "I think ... I think I'll be a café owner – cook nice greasy French fries, bum a few burgers ..." I saw the frown on his face and began to laugh. "You take everything so seriously," I said.

"Where you're concerned I do," he answered. Then he pulled

me closer and kissed me, right there in the parking lot. I'm sure Mrs Curlers next door was watching from behind her drapes, but I didn't really care. Grant and I were back together. One part of my life had not fallen apart. As the kiss went on, I remembered that I'd now kissed two boys within an hour. Was this a record? Then I wished that I hadn't remembered, because I couldn't help comparing Joe's kiss to Grant's. Strange emotions started churning inside me. Surely the wild, excited way I'd felt when I kissed Joe had only been part of the turmoil I was feeling? That kiss had been nothing more than an attempt to comfort me, right? Of course.

I broke away gently from Grant. "I'd ask you in," I told him, "but my mother is studying for a final tomorrow and I've got to cook her dinner."

"I understand," he said, looking at me tenderly. "I have a physics assignment to get started on anyway. I have to build a vehicle that runs on the energy of a mouse trap. I have no idea ..."

Poor old Grant, I thought as I waved to him. *He likes his world to be well ordered* and *predictable. He's not the type who would build cars out of mouse traps.* I let my mind drift to the kind of boy who would do something crazy like that. Strangely enough, the boy had a face a little like Joe's.

My mother was still at the kitchen table when I let myself in. I didn't know what to say, so I said, "I've got a chicken. I got it ready barbecued at the deli so we didn't have to cook it."

She nodded. "There's salad in the fridge," she said.

I started to prepare it, waiting all the time for the inevitable remark about my father not wanting me. But she didn't say more than a couple of words to me the whole time I was putting dinner together.

"If you don't mind, I'll go on studying while I eat," she said when I told her it was ready. "I still have so much to get through."

So I took my plate into my room and ate on a tray, watching

TV. I couldn't help noticing that while she had not said, "I told you so", she had also not seemed delighted to see me.

The next day she was still asleep when I left for school, so I left a note saying "Good luck with your exams" tacked to the fridge. I was nervous all day about seeing Joe again at the Heartbreak. I worried whether I had led him on at all or given him wrong signals by crying on his shoulder. What would happen if he now looked at me as his latest conquest? Worse still, what would happen if he bragged about it at the café? Joe was already there when I arrived. So was his grandfather.

"Hi!" I said cautiously.

Joe hardly looked up. "Don't tell me she made it in one piece today," he said. "No cars broken down, no giant waves on beaches – a miracle!"

"Why don't you leave the poor girl alone?" Mr Garbarini growled in his usual, fierce voice, giving him a thump on his back. "All the time you tease, tease, tease."

"That's because I'm trying to get her to quit," Joe said, "only she won't take the hint. She's a little slower about some things!" He looked up from the counter and just for a second our eyes held each other, then he grinned to himself and walked across the kitchen. "Besides," he said easily, "she's used to it. It's like those experiments with dogs. After they got used to those electric shocks, they couldn't live without them."

"Some electric shock," I retorted, feeling myself relax. "More like sleeping on a tack!" Then I remembered something. "And anyway, your month is up tomorrow, and since I'm not scheduled to work, it looks like you lost your bet – what a shame!"

"So I'll make a new bet for next month," he said.

"Over what?"

"You'll find out." And he grinned.

"You young people!" Mr Garbarini said, thumping down his

fist again. "Both as bad as the other. Why can't young people be kind and gentle to each other as kids were when I was young?"

"I thought you were always telling me how men were men when you were young, and how you were always fighting each other with knives?" Joe said with a wink at me. I was really glad things were back to normal again. It was hard enough to handle a gentle, considerate Grant without adding the complication of an involvement with Joe.

It was really nice to have Grant being sweet and attentive to me at school on Monday, because things sure weren't too pleasant at home. My mother was still super-tense over those exams. When I tried to ask her how she thought they went, she nearly bit my head off. So I was glad to escape to school next morning and glad to see Grant waiting for me at lunchtime.

"I wanted to ask you if you'd come to my tennis team awards banquet tomorrow night," he asked.

"You want me to come?" I asked. "I thought it was just for team members?"

"I just found out other guys are bringing girlfriends," he said. "I thought you'd like to see me get the trophy."

"I would," I said, "but I don't see how I can get out of work. Mr Garbarini's not coming in so there would be only Joe and me."

"Can't you switch with somebody?" Grant said sharply. "There's nobody to switch with. There's only Joe and me. It really takes two people, and it wouldn't be right to expect him to do all the work."

"Surely for once they can do without you?" Grant said, sounding bad-tempered now. "For something important like this?"

"I don't really see how …"

"Just don't show up. Call in sick or something," Grant said.

I glanced over at him. After all his talks about respecting me for wanting to lead my own life, he still took it for granted that I could get out of work whenever I felt like it. He obviously still thought my working in the café was a game or a joke, something that was not really as important as real life. It made me realize that I had grown up a little without really noticing it during the past few weeks.

"I'm sorry, Grant," I said. "I'd really love to come to your banquet, but I have to work at least until eight. I'll try to leave early and get to school for the awards part, so that I can see you get your trophy."

I could see he wasn't pleased about that, but he didn't push it any further. The next day I arrived at work, feeling a little bad about Grant sitting at his banquet without me, but very righteous that I had put duty first, like a character from history. Joe was chopping tomatoes furiously when I came in.

"Got to get everything done in a hurry today," he said, "because I want to split around eight."

"You what?" I asked, not liking what I thought I'd just heard.

He looked up at me and grinned. "Wendy," he said. "Wendy's folks are having a barbecue. It's her father's birthday. I couldn't say no to that, could I?"

"You want to clear out and leave me to run this place?" I demanded.

He looked just a little guilty. "I wouldn't do it ordinarily, but Wendy's folks insisted. Besides, you know how to run this place now. Just shows how much faith I've got in you."

"Your faith in me goes up and down like a yo-yo, depending on how much you want to flake off," I said.

"It does not," he said. "You know your stuff because you've had a great teacher!"

"Ha!" I said. "And what if I told you that I wanted to leave early tonight, too?"

"I'd say I'm the boss," he said. He grinned at me as I stomped past him into the kitchen. I wanted to tell him that I'd turned down an awards banquet at which my boyfriend was going to get a trophy just because I didn't think it was right to leave Joe working alone, and now he was walking out on me for a crummy evening with Wendy, but I saw it would do no good, so I suffered in silence.

The evening, as usual, started out busy. But by eight the food orders had subsided and we were down to mostly sodas and sundaes.

"I leave it in your capable hands," Joe said, taking off his uniform jacket.

"Can I have that in writing?" I asked, "or are you only saying my hands are capable because you want to leave with a clear conscience?"

He just laughed, ran a comb through his hair and went out, muttering, "Wendy, here I come ... wow!"

I managed just fine, thinking how far I had come in a few weeks. I really could run a restaurant single-handedly, and that was not bad. I had a real, marketable skill, which was one step better than my mother. I wondered if she was just using college as an escape from facing a real job.

I glanced up at the clock and saw it was almost nine. Grant's ceremony would be over. He'd probably be mad at me, thinking that I'd let him down and I didn't care. Just then a group of kids came in, all wanting hamburgers, fries, the works. So I was run off my feet, trying to cook four orders at once on my own. When I finally got them done, I was sweating and exhausted.

"Come sit down and have a soda," Art called as I walked past wearily. "I'm sure Howard's willing to pay, aren't you, Howie?"

"It's okay. I'll charge one to the house," I said, pouring myself one from the machine. "I deserve it tonight."

I sank gratefully on to the space on the bench Art had made for me. The talk was all about Joe and Wendy, and I didn't add much to the conversation until I heard Ashley say, "Are you still cooking something? It smells like something's burning in there."

"No," I said, puzzled. "I just served all the orders." I got up and walked back into the kitchen. The far corner was filled with black smoke.

"What is it?" Howard asked, breathing down my neck as usual.

"The French fryer," I said with a sigh. "It keeps overheating. We changed the thermostat, but it must be something more serious than that. I'd better unplug it at the wall."

"Be careful," Ashley warned. "I don't like the look of that smoke. Get down near the floor and crawl. That's what they say to do on TV."

I laughed. "That's only when you can't breathe," I said. "I can reach the wall sockets. No problem."

I was still a couple of yards away from the French fryer when it burst into a great whoomph of flame. A sheet of fire shot up to the ceiling and I could feel its heat from where I was standing. Everything seemed to switch into slow motion. I could hear Ashley's screams from behind me. In my brain an urgent voice was telling me to get out, right now, that there was nothing I could do and the café would burn down.

I'm in charge, I reminded myself uncertainly. *Joe left me in charge.*

I took Ashley's advice and crawled towards the wall, knocking out the plug.

I felt strong arms dragging me back.

"Are you crazy?" Art asked. "Let's get out of here!"

I turned and looked at the terrified faces behind me.

"We're going to be burned alive! We're going to be burned alive! I just know it!" Ashley was whimpering, clinging to Howard, which showed you how desperate she was.

Howard's eyes were glowing. "It's just like the movie *Firemen* when all those people are trapped in a blazing building. They don't burn up, though. They become these charred monsters."

"Ahhh!" Ashley wailed, dropping Howard's arm.

I decided someone had to do something quickly, and the only someone was me. "Look, let's not panic, okay?" I said, and I could hear my voice trembling. "We've still got customers in there. Art, you go call the fire department. Howard and Ashley, you get everybody out without a panic."

"Do you have a quarter?" Art asked.

"Give him one, Howard," I shouted.

"What about you?" Howard asked.

"I'm going to see if the fire extinguisher works," I said, taking it out of its bracket. My hands were shaking so much that I found it hard to focus on the directions. "Pull back ring pin. Hold upright. Aim nozzle at base of fire."

Beyond the kitchen door I could hear Howard's voice, "Don't get alarmed, anyone, but the whole kitchen has just gone up in flames and any minute now the whole building could go up and the ceiling could drop on you and you'll be trapped . . . But don't panic, okay?"

Then a lot of raised voices and fast-moving feet and Ashley's wail, "Howard, you made them leave before they paid!"

If I hadn't been so terrified, it would have been funny. I was still fumbling with the fire extinguisher. I couldn't even decide what the ring pin was for a moment, then I found myself actually aiming the nozzle. A huge white cloud came out, making me cough violently. My eyes were already stinging from the smoke. Now they streamed tears so that I could hardly see where I was aiming. I could hear spluttering and crackling but I just kept on aiming until the stream was getting weaker and weaker.

Right, I said to myself, eyeing the back door. *I've done my best and the fire's still not out. I hope Mr Garbarini and Joe know that I tried to save the café. There just wasn't enough in the fire extinguisher.*

I was feeling dizzy now from the smoke.

Get out right now, I warned myself. I staggered to the back door and stepped into the cold night air, just in time to see a red Alfa screech to a halt outside. Grant leaped out, strode towards the building and stopped when he saw me.

"Well, thanks for not showing up," he said angrily. "I just hope you have a really good excuse—"

I started to giggle. It was funny to think that the real world of awards banquets was still going on while a building was in the process of burning down.

He had stopped in midsentence and was staring at me. I suppose I looked quite a mess – all soot and grease and fire extinguishing stuff, giggling and staggering like an idiot. "Debbie?" he demanded. "What's going on?"

"It's my good excuse," I said. "I've just been fighting a fire." Then I must have swayed, because I remember Grant catching me, holding me in strong arms. He went to lower me on to the steps, then obviously became aware of what was still happening. "Oh, my God," he yelled. "There are flames in there?"

"Right," I said.

"Are you okay? Call the fire department! Let's get away from here!" he started to yell, in a very unherolike fashion. I wanted to tell him that this was not the way to behave for someone who has just won an award, but my head felt light and dizzy. I felt Grant lower me on to the steps. I was only dimly aware of the clanging of a siren as the first fire truck arrived and men in yellow slickers rushed up the steps.

Ten minutes later it was all out. Part of the wall and ceiling round the fryer was charred, but the building was still standing. One of the firemen came out.

"You kids did a great job in there," he said to the group that had assembled silently outside.

"It was Debbie! She did everything," Ashley said proudly. "She put out the fire and made us all get out."

I could see friendly faces smiling down at me, Howard's big grin and Art's cheeky smile and the others, all looking at me. Grant got to his feet. "Do you want me to drive you home?" he asked.

"I ought to stick around," I said. "I'm in charge here."

"Oh, for Pete's sake," he said. "You're obviously suffering from shock."

"I'm fine," I said. "I feel better now. I'll wait around. They've called the owner. You go on home, I'll be fine. You're all dressed up. You'll only get messy."

"I don't like to leave you here," he said, sounding undecided.

"These guys will take care of me, don't worry," I said. "I'll call you later," he said and climbed into his car. The crowd was still milling around. I sat on the steps again, feeling cold, while the firemen finished off in the kitchen, checking charred timbers and talking to headquarters. A reporter arrived from a local TV station. I answered questions, though I have no idea now what I said. Mr Garbarini arrived, yelling and waving his arms and stomping round his kitchen. When he heard the story he hugged me, almost crushing my ribs. I sat at one of the tables in the café, feeling very, very tired. All I wanted to do was go home, but I wasn't sure I could drive all the way up the hill. I wished I hadn't let Grant leave. Then, through all the noise in the kitchen, I could hear a new voice: "Where is she? Is she all right?" It was my mother, coming in to see me, her eyes wide with fear.

"Oh, thank heavens," she said when she saw me. "I just happened to turn on the ten o'clock news and they said a fire had gutted the café. Are you okay?"

I got unsteadily to my feet. "I'm fine," I said. "Just tired now and – Mom? I'm so glad you came."

She didn't say anything, but slipped an arm round my shoulder. "I'll take you home now," she said.

We had almost reached the front door when I heard a motorbike roar up and almost immediately afterwards, Joe's voice in the kitchen. "What happened? Where's Debbie? Is she okay?"

My mother opened the front door for us. I looked back to see Joe come running through. He stopped when he saw me and I could read the relief in his face. "Can't leave you five minutes without burning the place down, eh?" he asked.

"See you tomorrow," I said. "I'm going home."

"Sure. Run out and leave me to do the cleaning up," he said.

"What an unpleasant young man," my mother commented as we walked to her car. "Is he always that rude?"

"Always," I said, and grinned to myself as we drove up the hill.

After a shower had rinsed away most of the grease and soot, my mother tucked me in bed and sat awkwardly beside me.

"When I heard the news tonight," she began awkwardly, "and I thought I might lose you ..." Her voice choked and she couldn't go on.

I reached out to take her hand.

"I know we haven't been getting along too well," she said.

I nodded.

"I suppose I've been a little crabby," she said.

I laughed. "You can say that again."

"But it wasn't all me," she said.

I nodded again. "I suppose I've been feeling angry that things aren't the way they were," I said. "And I didn't think you had time for me any more. I didn't seem to matter to you."

She nodded. "The truth is," she said slowly, "that I've been so terrified about college that I haven't had time to notice what anyone else was feeling."

"Why were you so scared?" I asked.

"Because I didn't know whether I could do it," she said.

"Everyone else was fresh out of high school. They still knew how to study. I was terrified of finding out that I couldn't make it in college any more than I could make it in my marriage or the job market. I didn't want to find out I was a failure at everything."

"You're not a failure," I said, squeezing her hand.

"Everything's hard when you first try it. You should have seen the hamburgers I ruined. I even flipped one into the sink once, and one on to the window ledge."

"You did?" she asked, laughing.

"Yeah. Joe asked if I was ripening it in the sun," I said, laughing, too. "But now I cook them fine. And besides . . . you did a pretty good job with me. I'd say I turned out okay."

"You sure did," she said. "Come and give your old mother a hug." We were enveloped in each other's arms. I could smell her familiar sweet scent and buried my face in her shoulder. "I love you, Mom," I said.

"And I love you, too," she said. "Just give me a little more time to get my life back together, and I'll try to be a mother again, I promise."

"It's okay," I said. "I'll try to take over my share of things."

She held me away a little, so that we could look at each other. "It's been a tough time for both of us, hasn't it?" she asked.

I nodded. "I wouldn't like to go through this again too soon," I said. "But one good thing . . ."

"What's that?"

"Things can only get better, can't they?"

She began to laugh, holding me close again. "I hope so, darling. I really hope so!"

Heartbreak Café
2

THE MAIN ATTRACTION

JANET QUIN-HARKIN

Deborah Lesley's parents have split up. She and her mother live in a tiny apartment in a second-rate condominium, and Debbie's had to get an after school job as a waitress to earn extra money.

JOE GARBARINI is the manager of the Heartbreak Café – when he's not at school. He's super-cool, Mr Macho himself, and great on a motorbike. He and Debbie just DO NOT get on.

Movie-madness comes to Rockley Beach and the Heartbreak Café. The place is filled with kids trying to sign on as extras, and only Debbie and Joe seem to be unaffected – until Joe is asked to ride stunts on his motorbike, and he goes crazy too.

Debbie and Joe and Ashley and Howard and the rest of the gang are back again in the second book in the Heartbreak Café series by bestselling author Janet Quin-Harkin.

www.HeartbreakCafe.LA